GUESS WHO THIS FORTUNE SON IS SLEEPING WITH

Temperatures are rising in Sioux Falls—and so is the body heat....

In a town this small, secrets have a way of coming out. And do I have some dish for you! Turns out step-sibs Creed Fortune and Maya Blackstone may be getting a little too close for comfort as they comb the streets looking for her mother, Patricia. Everyone knows that Nash Fortune would do just about anything to get his missing wife back into his loving arms, but we wonder how he'd feel if he knew that there is hanky-panky going on between his "honorable" son and his virginal stepdaughter!

Apparently, Creed and Maya have had the hots for each other for several years. So we figure their legendary animosity is really just a smokescreen. You know what they say about forbidden fruit....

Dear Reader,

The time has finally come to say farewell to the Fortune family (at least this branch) in Heidi Betts's *Fortune's Forbidden Woman*. I hope you've been rooting for this couple to get together—I know I have. But just how are Creed and Maya going to get over the hurts they've caused one another? You'll just have to start reading to see!

This book also ties up several loose ends regarding Nash and Patricia. And hopefully it answers your questions about all five previous couples and where they are in their happily ever afters. Knowing the Fortune family, bliss is just around the corner.

Thank you for investing your time in this family and for your continued support of the Silhouette Desire line. And if you're anxious to meet a new family, join us next month for the launch of THE GARRISONS with Roxanne St. Claire's *The CEO'S Scandalous Affair*. I think you'll love this Miami family and all the exotic romances they are about to embark on.

Melissa Jeglinski

Melissa Jeglinski
Senior Editor
Silhouette Desire

Please address questions and book requests to:
Silhouette Reader Service
U.S.: 3010 Walden Ave., P.O. Box 1325, Buffalo, NY 14269
Canadian: P.O. Box 609, Fort Erie, Ont. L2A 5X3

HEIDI BETTS

FORTUNE'S FORBIDDEN WOMAN

Published by Silhouette Books
America's Publisher of Contemporary Romance

For Mom—because it's been a while. I love you!

Special thanks and acknowledgment are given
to Heidi Betts for her contribution
to the DAKOTA FORTUNES miniseries.

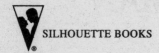 SILHOUETTE BOOKS

ISBN-13: 978-0-373-76801-1
ISBN-10:   0-373-76801-X

FORTUNE'S FORBIDDEN WOMAN

Copyright © 2007 by Harlequin Books S.A.

Books by Heidi Betts

Silhouette Desire

Bought by a Millionaire #1638
Blame It on the Blackout #1662
When the Lights Go Down #1686
Seven-Year Seduction #1709
Mr. and Mistress #1723
Bedded Then *Wed* #1761
Blackmailed into Bed #1779
Fortune's Forbidden Woman #1801

HEIDI BETTS

An avid romance reader since junior high school, Heidi knew early on that she wanted to write these wonderful stories of love and adventure. It wasn't until her freshman year of college, however, when she spent the entire night reading a romance novel instead of studying for finals, that she decided to take the road less traveled and follow her dream. In addition to reading and writing romance, she is the founder of her local Romance Writers of America chapter and has a tendency to take injured and homeless animals of every species into her Central Pennsylvania home.

Heidi loves to hear from readers. You can write to her at P.O. Box 99, Kylertown, PA 16847 (an SASE is appreciated, but not necessary) or e-mail heidi@heidibetts.com. And be sure to visit www.heidibetts.com for news and information about upcoming books.

THE DAKOTA FORTUNES

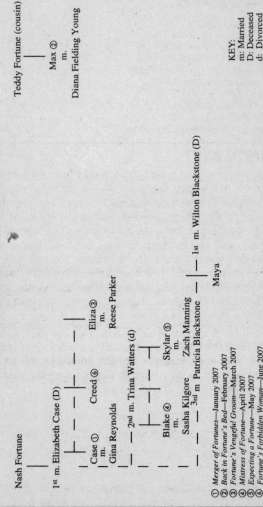

Nash Fortune

Teddy Fortune (cousin)

1st m. Elizabeth Case (D)

Max ②
m.
Diana Fielding Young

Case ①
m.
Gina Reynolds

Eliza ③
m.
Reese Parker

Creed ⑥

2nd m. Trina Watters (d)

Blake ④
m.
Sasha Kilgore

Skylar ⑤
m.
Zach Manning

3rd m Patricia Blackstone ——— 1st m. Wilton Blackstone (D)

Maya

① *Merger of Fortunes*—January 2007
② *Back in Fortune's Bed*—February 2007
③ *Fortune's Vengeful Groom*—March 2007
④ *Mistress of Fortune*—April 2007
⑤ *Expecting a Fortune*—May 2007
⑥ *Fortune's Forbidden Woman*—June 2007

KEY:
m: Married
D: Deceased
d: Divorced

One

"Thank you for dinner," Maya Blackstone said as she fitted her key into the lock of her downtown Sioux Falls town house. She twisted the key and then the knob, opening the door a crack before turning back to Brad McKenzie.

It was dark outside, but the yellow glow of the porch light reflected his tall frame, chestnut hair and handsome face.

"You're welcome," he said, offering a small smile as his hand stroked down her arm, left bare by the sleeveless knit top she was wearing. "Aren't you going to invite me in?"

Gooseflesh broke out along her skin, making her shiver. She shouldn't have been surprised by his suggestion. They'd been dating for almost a year now, and Brad was one of the nicest guys she'd ever met. It was only natural that their relationship would begin to move in a more physical, intimate direction. Lord knew he'd been pushing for it for months now.

Not aggressively, and not in any way that would make her feel pressured, but she wasn't stupid. She knew what all the little touches and caresses meant. She also knew that most couples who'd been seeing each other as long as she and Brad had would already be sleeping together.

And there was no reason she *shouldn't* go to bed with him. He was kind, good-looking, successful and treated her like a princess. She was even attracted to him.

So what was her problem? What was she waiting for?

Taking a deep breath, she steeled her nerves and made her decision.

"Of course." Pushing open the front door, she stepped inside and flipped on the light that illuminated the small entryway. She set her purse on the decorative bench she kept against the wall and headed for the kitchen, leaving Brad to close the door and follow along. He'd been inside her house often enough to know his way around and make himself at home.

"Would you like something to drink?" she asked, going to the refrigerator to see what she had to offer. "Iced tea or a glass of wine. I could make some coffee."

He came up behind her, standing so close she could feel the heat of his body at her back.

"Wine would be good," he murmured in a low voice, taking the opportunity to rub her shoulders.

Fighting the urge to shrug away from his hold, she grabbed the open bottle of chardonnay from the top shelf of the refrigerator, then opened a nearby cupboard to retrieve two glasses. She walked around the corner into the living room, breaking Brad's hold on her but knowing he was close on her heels.

They lowered themselves onto the overstuffed, floral-patterned sofa. Maya sat forward, setting the glasses on the coffee table while she popped the cork and poured a generous amount of the fragrant liquid for each of them.

She turned to hand one of the glasses to Brad, taking a deep breath to keep from shifting farther away. He was sitting close, his thigh pressing along hers, his shoulder brushing her own as he took the wine.

This was ridiculous, she chastised herself. What was she afraid of? What was she waiting for?

Brad sipped his wine while she drank hers a bit more forcefully, then set her empty glass on the table in front of them. Turning, she smiled and settled against his side, both of them leaning into the soft back of the sofa.

His brows lifted, and it took a second for his arm to tighten around her.

She didn't blame him for being surprised, since she wasn't usually the one to make the first move.

Usually? Try never. She had never made the first move with Brad. A part of her couldn't believe she was doing it now.

But a year was long enough. She *wanted* to be with Brad. She wanted to be normal, have a normal relationship. And if things were ever going to move forward with them, become more serious, she needed to get over these intimacy issues she seemed to have.

Tipping her head back, she silently invited him to kiss her. An invitation he wasted no time accepting.

Despite her reservations, she had to admit he was a good kisser. Even she had no trouble recognizing that aspect of his personality.

His mouth moved over hers smoothly, his lips warm and firm. He caressed her shoulders, then her arms, his hands sliding around to her back.

It felt good, enjoyable, and she thought they really might make it this time.

With a moan he pulled her closer, deepening the kiss and pressing their bodies together so that she could feel the clear sign of his arousal.

Her stomach clenched, but not with desire. Nerves flared to life in her bloodstream, her muscles growing tense, her breathing growing labored as panic set in.

Dammit. She stiffened, whimpering partly in fear and partly in aggravation as she put out her arms and shoved away.

Brad blinked, his chest heaving, stunned by her sudden retreat.

"I'm sorry," she said, shaking her head and shifting back as far as she could against the arm of the couch.

Why, *why* did she keep doing this? Why couldn't she

act like a regular twenty-five-year-old woman and sleep with her boyfriend without being plagued by so many doubts? Without seeing *his* face when she closed her eyes, and hearing *his* voice thundering in her ears.

Damn, damn, damn.

Brad blew out a breath and ran his fingers through his hair, frustration rolling off of him in waves. "I know. You're sorry, but you can't."

The words held no accusation or anger whatsoever, which only made her feel worse.

When he got to his feet, she jumped up and followed him across the room toward the front door.

"I really am sorry," she told him, feeling guilty and miserable, but not knowing what else to say.

What else *could* she say? She *was* sorry, even though she couldn't offer him any more of an explanation than that.

At the door he paused with his hand on the knob and turned to meet her gaze. She thought he must surely be entertaining thoughts of chewing her out at this point, but his hazel eyes remained soft and gentle.

"I know you are. So am I." He lifted a hand to tuck a loose strand of hair behind her ear. "I told you I wouldn't push you, Maya, and I meant it. I'm becoming a pro at cold showers," he added with a tiny lift to his lips, "but no pressure."

Stepping onto the front stoop, he turned back to kiss her cheek before walking slowly back to his car.

She watched him drive away, then closed the door

and banged her head lightly on the cool wood a few times. Even she was getting tired of this, so she could just imagine how poor Brad was feeling. She only wished there was something she could do about the anxieties that were turning memories from the past into a full-blown phobia.

It was all *his* fault. She hadn't seen her step-brother in months, but still Creed Fortune somehow managed to be the plague of her existence.

Ever since she was a little girl, when she and her mother had moved into the Fortune Estate so Patricia could act as nanny to Nash Fortune's four young children, Creed had been nothing but cold to her. Even after Nash and her mother had fallen in love and married, making Nash's kids Maya's new stepsiblings, she had still gotten along with the others better than she had with Creed.

It was easy to be friends with Skylar, who was only a year older than Maya. They'd had a lot in common and had played together from the time they were little.

Eliza had been six years older and not much inter-ested in playing role model to another girl other than her own half sister, though she'd always been nice to Maya. And Blake—Skylar's brother and Nash's son from his second marriage to Trina Watters—had thank-fully been kind to her.

But Case and Creed Fortune—sons from Nash's first marriage to his now deceased college sweetheart, Eliz-abeth—were several years older than Maya and had always treated her like an outsider. They'd ignored her and made her feel unwelcome in what was supposed to be her own home.

She'd never really been comfortable living in that big house with so many people who were technically her family but felt more like strangers.

In addition, Maya had always been the ugly stepsister. She was plain and quiet, and not a true Fortune. She was simply the shy, unremarkable girl who'd shown up one day with the new, live-in nanny and ended up a sister when their parents fell in love. But that didn't mean any of the *real* Fortune children had to like her.

Pushing away from the door, she dragged herself back to the living room to collect the wineglasses and nearly empty bottle. When she reached the kitchen, she put Brad's glass upside down over one of the spokes of the dishwasher basket, then poured the end of the wine into her own glass, watching the last few drops *drip, drip, drip* as her head began to pound.

And after all of the insecurities and loneliness, she'd still been crazy enough to develop a childhood crush on Creed almost from the moment she met him. He'd been handsome, older…and so sophisticated.

He was still handsome, older and sophisticated…but she'd long ago given up on winning his heart.

Honestly, she'd have had better luck attracting the attention of a fence post. No matter how often she followed him around or how many cow-eyed glances she'd sent him, he'd never given her the time of day. If anything, he'd only grown colder and more distant the longer her crush had lingered on.

It was highly humiliating. And what made matters even worse was the fact that she apparently *still* wasn't over him.

Was she in love with him?

She didn't think so. She certainly didn't want to be.

But she also couldn't seem to get him out of her brain. He swirled in there, making her neurotic and half-insane.

She was mature enough to realize that the case of puppy love she'd entertained as a kid had been nothing more than a sick case of hero worship. Unfortunately, that hero worship had since worked itself into a maddening and unhealthy obsession with Creed Fortune.

Which was hopeless and futile, considering he'd never shown the least bit of interest in her as a woman. He'd never shown the least bit of interest in her, period.

Yet he still managed to intrude on her self-confidence, her sexuality and her relationship with Brad.

With a growl Maya threw back the last of the wine, added her own glass to the dishwasher basket, then slammed the appliance door closed. She swore, if Creed were standing in front of her right this minute, she'd be sorely tempted to slap him.

Taking a deep breath, she turned on her heel and headed for the stairs. What she needed was a hot shower and a solid eight hours of sleep.

What she *didn't* need was this flood of doubts and frustrations. For God's sake, her life was already complicated enough without adding a lukewarm romance and painful memories to the mix.

Instead of worrying about her love life, she ought to be concerned about her mother.

Patricia had been missing for six weeks now. No one had a clue where she was or what had caused her to leave. All they knew was that one day she was there and the next she wasn't.

Poor Nash was beside himself, frantic and confused, not knowing what had driven Patricia away, but desperate to find her.

Maya was equally upset, and couldn't imagine why her mother would have taken off the way she did. True, Patricia had seemed somewhat distracted over the past few months, but Maya had never expected it to lead to anything like this.

Her mother's disappearance was the main reason she'd been out with Brad tonight. Nash had immediately hired private detectives to try to track down Patricia, so there was very little Maya could do except wait and worry. Thoughts of her mother had her completely preoccupied, even during work days, when she should be concentrating on educating the young minds of her grade-school students.

And because Brad was kind and considerate and thoughtful, he understood what she was going through and wanted to help however he could—mainly by keeping her busy with dinners out, long drives, even the occasional cultural events.

It was one more reason she cared for Brad and was so angry with herself for not being able to take their relationship to the next level.

She was halfway up the stairs and still steaming when the phone rang. With a grumble she turned around and moved to answer the kitchen extension rather than race the rest of the way up the steps to her bedroom.

"Hello?" she all but snapped.

"Maya?" a deep male voice replied, as though the caller wasn't sure she was the one who'd answered the phone. "It's Creed."

She knew who it was. If there was one voice she could identify over all others on the planet, it was Creed Fortune's.

"What do you want, Creed?" she asked none too politely.

Of course she already knew. He'd been calling on a regular basis to check on her ever since her mother went missing.

Why he bothered, Maya couldn't fathom. He certainly hadn't given a fig about her the past thirteen years he'd known her.

"I just wanted to see how you're holding up. The detectives Nash hired haven't turned up anything on your mom yet, but I'm sure they will soon."

"How am I holding up?" she repeated, her annoyance with both him and herself flaring to life again and coming out in the razor sharpness of her tone. "How am I holding up? Oh, I'm fine. Just peachy. Damn you, Creed."

Her fingers tightened on the handset and she began to pace back and forth across the kitchen, as far as the spiral cord would allow.

"This is all your fault. You've ruined my chances of ever having a normal relationship with a man, ever *sleeping* with a man. You blamed a seventeen-year-old girl for being attacked by her boyfriend and called me a slut. You're the reason I can't have a normal relationship, and I hate you for that!"

Her tirade ended with her voice at least one octave higher than usual. Without giving him a chance to respond, she slammed the phone down, muttered a low curse, and marched off to bed.

It was almost midnight and the windows were dark, but Creed Fortune couldn't have cared less. He stomped up the steps to Maya's town house and pounded on the door with the side of his fist.

To hell with the doorbell. To hell with the fact that she was probably sound asleep. He wanted to talk to her, and he wanted to do it *now*.

Where did she get off telling *him* he'd ruined her for ever going to bed with a man?

She sure hadn't had any trouble attracting the opposite sex in high school, not once she'd begun to fill out with those soft, feminine curves and grown into her striking half-Yankton-Sioux features. The long, black hair, chocolate-brown doe eyes and ripe little body had had boys panting after her like a mare in heat.

He pounded again, louder and longer this time. Across the street a dog barked, and inside he thought he heard movement. A second later a light flicked on and the door swung open.

He took a moment to hope she'd checked the peephole first, then rational thought spun away as he took in her tousled hair, drowsy eyes and the short, faded nightshirt that seemed to cling in all the right places.

With a tired sigh, she leaned against the edge of the door and let her lashes flutter to half-mast. "Now what do you want, Creed? In case you hadn't noticed, it's the middle of the night and *some people* are trying to sleep."

"At least we know you're sleeping alone, don't we?"

A spark flashed in her narrowed eyes. "Go to hell," she said, and made a move to slam the door in his face.

He stuck out his booted foot, blocking the motion. It didn't keep her from pressing forward and throwing her body against the heavy wood.

"Get your foot out of the door, Creed. Go bother someone else and let me go back to bed."

He added his knee and upper body to the battle, causing her to grunt as he pushed her back and forced his way into the house. Kicking the door closed behind him, he leaned against it and crossed his arms over his chest. Maya did the same, retreating several steps until she'd put what he was sure she felt was a safe distance between them.

"Adding forced entry to your résumé these days?" she asked belligerently.

He shrugged, keeping his face blank even as heat started to pump through his blood and pool near the region of his groin. Dammit, why did she have to be so beautiful?

She was his stepsister, for God's sake. Not related by blood in any way, but related through the marriage of his father to her mother.

No matter how you cut it, she was forbidden fruit, and he had no business lusting after her. No business at all.

Never mind that he'd secretly been doing just that since she'd hit puberty. He was ten years too old for her, and supposed to play the part of big brother, but still he'd wanted her.

Why did she have to grow up in so many interesting places? Why couldn't she have remained a plain and gawky child forever?

Tamping down his errant thoughts, he kicked away from the door and headed toward her. "If I have to," he said in answer to her question.

"What are you doing, Creed?" She continued her backward shuffle, occasionally bumping into the wall or glancing behind her to make sure the path was clear. "Why are you here?"

"Do I need a reason?" he asked, never breaking eye contact.

"Yes. You do. Have you found out something about

my mother? If so, tell me and then get out. Otherwise, just get out."

They both stopped moving. One corner of his mouth lifted in a humorless half grin. Since when had she become so good at telling him off and ordering him around? It certainly was a change from the quiet, meek girl she'd been when they were kids.

"No, nothing about your mother. The private investigators are still working on it. I'm here because of what you said on the phone."

Her expression flickered, the hard, angry glint in her eyes being replaced by wary uncertainty. He even thought he saw a touch of pink color her high cheekbones.

"*I* ruined you for other men?" he pressed. "Just what the hell is that supposed to mean?"

She flinched. A small, almost imperceptible motion, and the only sign that she was uncomfortable with the topic of conversation. But he caught it, and some part of him reveled in his ability to shake her.

"Nothing." Her voice was low and she gave one quick, jerky shake of her head. "It doesn't mean anything. I was tired and worried about my mom. I didn't know what I was saying."

Valiant effort, but he didn't buy it.

He took another step forward. "Guess that means Brad isn't getting any, huh? Nearly a year of sniffing around your skirts, and he gets nothing for his trouble. Poor, pathetic loser."

Her chin went up at that, her shoulders squaring as

she straightened her spine. "Look who's talking. I may not be sleeping with Brad, he may not be 'getting any,' but at least he's a gentleman. He would never barge into my house and corner me like this. He would never accuse me of being a tramp, or make me feel like one the way you did just because a boy sweet-talked me into his car when I was seventeen and then *attacked me.*"

It was his turn to flinch, but only on the inside. He remembered that night as though it were yesterday. Stumbling upon Maya and her current boyfriend—or at least one of the boys she'd been hanging out with quite a bit that summer, ever since the opposite sex had begun to take notice of her fine feminine form... Taking notice of the tell-tale rocking of the shiny Trans Am and the noises that were emanating from inside...and then realizing Maya's cries weren't of the pleasurable variety.

He remembered the fury he'd felt as he'd opened the driver's side door and yanked the boy out by the scruff of his neck. The kid—some varsity football jock with a letterman jacket—had been lucky to get away with only a few scrapes and bruises, because Creed had sincerely considered killing the little bastard.

As it was, he'd given the jerk a beating he wouldn't soon forget. Then he'd dragged Maya home, filling her ears with lectures and invectives the whole way.

"That's why you won't sleep with Brad McKenzie?" He made a scoffing sound, his mouth twisting into a wry smirk. "He must not be very persuasive. I could have you begging for it in two seconds flat."

Any intimidation or discomfort Maya might have been feeling flew out the window at his cocky remark. Her brown eyes glittered dangerously and every muscle in her body went rigid. She'd been backed up until her calves hit the edge of the sofa, but now she took a single, confident step forward.

"Oh, really. And just how would you manage that? Twist my arm until I told you what you wanted to hear, whether it was true or not?"

Her words were like gasoline thrown on an already raging brush fire. The low-level desire humming through his system suddenly ratcheted up several notches to full, mind-numbing throttle.

He reached out, taking her by the wrist and tugging her against his chest.

"No," he breathed. "Like this."

And then he took her mouth with his.

Two

For a moment Maya froze, so stunned her mind went blank and her body refused to move. But Creed's lips were firm, his body hot, his arms like steel bands where he held her tight against him.

Her eyes slid closed and her fingers curled into his shoulders, kneading like a kitten. She moaned.

How long had she dreamed of this? Of having him kiss her, hold her, *want* her.

Forever, that's how long. Since she and her mother had moved into the Fortune Estate and she'd first been introduced to the brooding, much older young man who towered over and intimidated her. Even as a shy, somewhat awkward girl, she'd known her own heart, and her heart had wanted Creed Fortune.

But she'd never truly believed she could have him. Not when he took every opportunity to make it clear she was nothing but a thorn in his side. An uninvited sibling, forced upon him by an unexpected romance between his father and her mother.

Now, though…now she knew she'd been wrong. He'd done a good job of hiding it, but apparently he shared her feelings and wanted her as much as she'd always wanted him.

His kiss was sweltering, raising her temperature and causing her to break out in beads of perspiration. He worked her mouth as if she was a decadent dessert and he couldn't get enough.

Tongues tangled, teeth nipped and clashed. She pressed herself close to his tall frame, letting her breasts brush the solid wall of his chest, the insistent bulge of his arousal nudge the space between her legs.

This was better than anything she'd ever experienced. Better than any other kiss she'd shared with any other man. Better even than all the times over the past year that she'd tried to relax enough to make love with Brad, but ended up pulling back at the last minute.

It was better, she knew, because it was Creed. And with him she wasn't afraid, she wasn't shy, she wasn't self-conscious.

With him she didn't recall his long-ago accusation that she acted like a slut, but instead remembered all the times she'd wanted him, lusted after him, dreamed about him.

And now, finally, she could have him.

Her arms tightened around his neck, her fingers playing in the ends of his short, dark brown hair. She whimpered and wiggled in his hold, striving desperately for something she couldn't name.

He pulled away, chest heaving, breathing ragged. His blue eyes glittered as he held her gaze.

Muttering a heartfelt curse, he shook his head, then swooped in to take her mouth again.

This time he didn't settle for just kissing. His hands clasped her waist and swung her around, manipulating her as easily as a tailor's mannequin. Without breaking the contact of their lips and tongues, he walked her backward through the living room and hall, up the staircase and into her bedroom.

She didn't stop to wonder how he knew his way through her house or which bedroom was hers; she was simply relieved by his focus and excellent navigational skills. And she clung to him, wrapping her legs around his waist halfway up the stairs to aid his progress.

He carried her into the room and straight to the bed, laying her on top of the covers, rumpled from where she'd thrown them off when he'd woken her with his pounding.

Her nightshirt bunched to her waist, the rough denim of his jeans rubbing against the soft skin of her inner thighs. His hands sneaked over her hips and waist, beneath the hem of the shirt, pushing it higher as his fingers moved toward the swells of her breasts.

His lips caressed her chin and jawline, brushing the lobe of her ear before trailing down her throat in a series of nips and licks. When she felt a gentle pressure beneath her arms, she lifted them willingly above her head and let him pull the nightshirt off entirely.

The cool evening air blew across her naked breasts and torso, and she quickly lowered her hands to cover herself.

"Don't."

Creed's fingers circled her wrists like manacles, slowly tugging her hands away to reveal her nudity to his hungry gaze.

"Don't hide," he said again, his voice low and strained. "I want to see you, all of you."

He ran the side of his thumb over the tip of one breast, grinning when it puckered and swelled beneath his ministrations.

She sucked in a breath of air, her back arching into his touch. Her face felt flushed, her entire body a wriggling mass of fever-hot nerve endings, even as she fought not to let her natural tendency toward embarrassment take over.

He had her hands pinned above her head, the rest of her pinned by his weight and bulk. And the look in his eyes was that of a hungry wolf—fierce, predatory, determined.

"Lovely," he murmured, then swooped in to lick a tight, budded nipple.

She gasped, her fingers clenching into fists above where he held her arms down. He licked the other nipple, just a quick, light swipe, before settling in with more thorough, undivided attention.

His tongue rasped like sandpaper along her sensitive nerve endings. He turned her flesh hot with his mouth, then cool with the soft hush of his breath. After creating a world of sensual devastation at one breast, he moved to the other and did it all over again.

When he lifted his head, he was grinning. "Like I said, lovely."

His fingers loosened from her wrists, but she didn't bother attempting to lower her arms. She didn't have the strength, even if she'd wanted to. She simply lay there like a rag doll, depleted of energy or the will to move.

Still smiling, he skimmed the underside of her arms, the sides of her breasts, her waist, until he reached the top of her high-cut bikini panties. They were nothing special, just plain lavender cotton. But then, she hadn't known anyone would be seeing them when she'd dressed for bed a few hours ago.

Her choice of undergarments didn't seem to bother Creed, though. He brushed his lips around her navel and along the waistband of the panties, then slowly began to drag them off.

A flutter of self-consciousness rippled in her belly, and she had to curl her fingers into the sheets to keep from covering herself again or trying to wiggle away.

If Creed noticed her sudden bout of discomfort, he didn't acknowledge it. Instead, he kept his gaze locked on the dark triangle at the apex of her thighs that he was revealing inch by agonizing inch. He pushed the panties down her legs, slipping them over her feet and letting them fall to the floor beside the bed.

A moment later he pushed to his feet and straightened, all six feet, two inches looming above her.

For a second Maya thought he meant to leave…leave her there, naked and flushed, and walk away. But then his arms lifted and his fingers began to deftly release the line of buttons at the front of his shirt.

One by one, he slipped them through their holes, and little by little his chest became exposed. The bronzed skin. The firm muscles. The light sprinkling of dark hair.

Maya's mouth went dry and she had trouble breathing. He was so beautiful. Tall, athletic, sculpted like some sort of Greek god, or the epitome of the perfect man every woman fantasized about.

He was certainly her idea of the perfect man.

Tugging the tails of his shirt out of the waistband of his jeans, he released the last couple buttons before shrugging out of the shirt and letting it drop to the floor. He started to kick off his boots, at the same time unzipping his trousers.

He pushed everything, jeans and underwear, down his legs and off. But instead of leaving them in a pile on the floor, he withdrew a rear pocket, pulled out his wallet, then dug out a small plastic square. Dropping the clothes, he stepped intently back to the bed in all his naked glory.

He was the first man she'd ever seen completely nude, but for once, she wasn't flushed with embarrassment. She was…awed.

Amazing didn't quite cover it. Neither did *fabulous, marvelous,* or any of the other two hundred adjectives that flitted through her mind. A few of her more precocious students might say *hubba-hubba,* and that came close.

His shoulders were broad, his waist flat and tapering down to narrow hips, his legs long and well-muscled. But it was what hung between those legs that held her rapt attention.

Admittedly, her experience of such things was limited. Limited, ha! Verging on nonexistent, was more like it. But even so, she was familiar with the basics of the male anatomy, and in her somewhat biased opinion, Creed was a most impressive specimen.

Before she had a chance to look her fill, he was stretching out above her, covering her from head to toe. The hair on his legs and chest tickled, but she didn't laugh. She was too distracted by the rigid length of his erection rubbing her in all the right places.

His fingers drifted over her temples, threading through her hair to hold her steady while he planted light, butterfly kisses on either side of her mouth. First one corner, then the other before he took her mouth for a slow, luxurious exploration. He made her feel like a particularly decadent sweet he wanted to take his time with and really enjoy.

While he continued to kiss her deeply, his hands

traveled down her body, one pausing to toy with the tip of her breast, the other sliding lower. Past her waist, over the curve of her buttock, and down her thigh until he reached the bend of her knee.

He lifted her leg, bringing it up to hook around his hip so he could settle more fully against her. His arousal, already sheathed in the condom he'd retrieved from his wallet, prodded her feminine opening.

Cocking her hips, she opened herself even wider, doing everything she could to ease his entry. He slipped inside, just the tip, but she was already wet and ready for him. She'd been waiting for this moment all her life, and her body was primed and more than eager for him to finally claim her.

A low groan rolled up from his diaphragm as he pressed deeper. Inch by inch, he filled her, stretching her slick inner folds until she thought she could die from the sheer pleasure of it all.

Just when she figured he couldn't go any farther, he pushed forward again. This time, instead of pleasure, a sharp, lightning flash of pain made her stiffen and bite her bottom lip to keep from crying out.

Thankfully, the discomfort passed quickly, and she was once again able to breathe. Above her, Creed held himself perfectly still, staring down at her. His brows knit in consternation.

"Are you all right?"

The words were strained, his chest heaving as he struggled to get enough air into his lungs. The muscles in his biceps quivered with the effort to hold his weight off her.

She nodded, offering a small smile to let him know she was telling the truth. A beat passed while he considered her answer, then seemed to take her at her word.

He returned his mouth to hers, kissing her softly but thoroughly while lower, he began a slow in and out motion that washed away any lingering tenderness. Instead, there was only pleasure.

It started as just a trickle, the temporary replacement of something not-so-nice with something not-so-bad. But soon enough the sensation grew, building in ever-increasing waves.

She lifted her legs to lock more tightly around his waist, urging him closer. Her hands smoothed up and down his back, the nails alternately digging in and clawing long lines across the sweat-slickened flesh.

His own fingers clasped her bottom, kneading and stroking as his thrusts picked up speed. He moved deeper, harder, faster, until she was gasping against his mouth and reaching for…she didn't know what. She only knew she wanted it, needed it, might die without it.

Still holding her hip and buttock, Creed's other hand slipped between them and stole into her damp folds, finding the tiny bud of desire hidden within. He rubbed the spot, first lightly, then with more pressure, making her cry out and writhe beneath him.

"Come with me," he whispered raggedly. The rough

line of his cheek abraded hers, his lips mere inches from her ear. "Come with me *now*."

He pounded into her again, at the same time his fingers worked their magic, sending her off like a rocket. Her mouth opened on a soundless scream, her back arched and her vision went hazy.

From somewhere outside her body, she felt him thrust once, twice more and then stiffen above her. Oxygen left his lungs in a loud sigh as he collapsed, his weight pressing her down into the mattress.

She lay there, her legs still wrapped around his waist, her arms still linked about his shoulders and a smile as wide as the Big Sioux River curving her lips.

Making love with Creed Fortune was everything she'd ever imagined and more. It had fulfilled every one of her adolescent fantasies, not to mention more than a few of the hopes and dreams she'd envisioned since becoming an adult.

For the first time, she was glad she hadn't slept with another man, even Brad. She hadn't realized what she was really doing all those years, but she'd inadvertently been saving herself for Creed, and for that she could never be sorry.

She knew better than to think everything would be perfect from this moment on. Creed wasn't going to ask her to marry him in the next five minutes, or declare his undying love.

This was a start, though. They may have put the cart before the horse in their personal relationship by sleeping together before they'd ever even been out on a date, but there was time for all of that.

Time to get to know each other better—really get to know each other. Time to go out, have fun and get the family used to the idea that they were going to be together.

It would come as quite a surprise to the Fortunes, she imagined, including her mother. But they all loved her and Creed, and as long as they were happy, she knew they would offer their support wholeheartedly. She hoped so, anyway.

The important thing was that this was the beginning. The beginning of everything she'd ever wanted, and for the first time, she realized she could have it.

Delight coursed through her veins and her grin widened. It was all she could do to keep from giggling aloud.

She couldn't remember ever being so happy. And she would make Creed happy, too, she swore she would.

Above her, he shifted slightly, slipping out of her and rolling to his side. Cool air brushed the perspiration dotting her skin, and she immediately missed his weight, his warmth.

With a groan, he sat up, rubbed his fingers through his hair, then stood and headed for the adjoining bathroom. She heard the water running for a second, then he was back, in all his naked glory. He stalked across the room, and she took the opportunity to admire him every step of the way.

Expecting him to rejoin her, she shimmied toward the head of the bed, rearranging the pillows and crawling under the covers, leaving plenty of room for him to crawl in beside her. They would probably cuddle a bit first, maybe take a nap, then hopefully make love all over again. She couldn't wait.

Instead he bypassed the bed altogether, bending to retrieve his jeans from the floor. Without a word he stepped into them, adding his shirt and boots in short order.

Her brows met in a frown. "What are you doing?"

He didn't bother to meet her gaze as he finished buttoning the pine-green shirt, tucking it into the waistband of his pants.

"I'm leaving."

"Leaving?" Clutching the sheet to her breasts, she scrambled forward, climbing to her knees. "What do you mean you're leaving? I thought…" She'd thought so many things, but she settled for, "I thought you'd at least stay the night."

"Why would I stay? Now that I've gotten you out of my system, I can leave you alone. Get on with my life."

He finished rolling the sleeves of his shirt to just below the elbows, finally glancing in her direction. "Good night, Maya."

Then he turned and walked out of the bedroom.

She could hear his footsteps in the hall, pounding down the steps and through the rest of the house. A second later the front door slammed, sending a shiver down her spine.

She sat frozen, unable to believe what had just happened. He'd made love to her, made her believe he cared, that they had a future together, and then walked out. He'd gotten dressed and walked out as if she meant nothing to him.

She felt stunned, her heart squeezing painfully inside her chest.

Drawing her knees up, she buried her face in the wrinkled sheet and wept.

Chase stood on Maya's front porch, leaning against the closed door with his eyes tightly closed.

He hoped she didn't chase after him. He didn't want to see her again, not right now.

For one thing, there was nothing left to say. It might have sounded harsh, but what he'd told her back in her bedroom was the absolute truth: succumbing to his baser instincts meant he could move past the almost obsessive longing he'd always felt when he was near her.

Now that he'd been with her, the mystery was solved. Any questions he might have been harboring about what she would look like naked, how her skin would feel beneath his hands and mouth, what sounds she would make when he was inside her, had been answered.

For another, he wasn't entirely sure he could look at her right now and not be sorely tempted to make love to her again. He was a man, after all, and the last he'd seen Maya, she hadn't been wearing anything more than a thin white sheet, which would be easy enough to dispense with.

Shaking off erotic images that were beginning to reheat his blood, he pushed away from the door and headed for his car.

What the hell had gotten into him, to touch her at all? How could he have let things get so out of control?

He'd wanted her for a decade, lusted after her in a way no stepbrother had any business lusting. But he'd never, ever intended to act on those desires, and he thought he'd done a pretty good job of hiding them from Maya and everyone else.

Starting the engine, he flipped on the headlights and pulled away from the curb, heading home. He needed a good night's sleep, and maybe a nice, stiff drink to clear his head and make sense of what he'd done not twenty minutes before.

She was off-limits. Forbidden. She always had been. If they'd ever crossed the lines of impropriety, the scandal would have been huge.

He took a hand off the wheel, scrubbing it roughly over his face. Dammit, it would *be* huge, if anyone ever found out what had taken place tonight.

Which meant it couldn't happen. No one could find out.

He would never intentionally do anything to bring shame or undue attention to his family, so he certainly wasn't going to tell anyone. And he doubted Maya would, either.

So all he had to do now was keep his hands to himself.

Using his pass key, he opened the electronic gate of the underground garage at the Dakota Fortune office building and pulled his dark-blue Mercedes S-class into his personal parking spot near the elevators. His brother Case had a reserved space right beside his own, but except during business hours, it mostly stood empty these days.

The same could be said of Case's apartment, across the hall from Creed's. The top floor of Dakota Fortune had been split into two separate living areas, which the brothers had occupied after moving out of the Fortune Estate and taking over as copresidents for the family company.

Of course, Case was now happily set up in a house just outside Sioux Falls with his wife, Gina. She'd inherited her childhood home when her father died, and after living in an apartment in town for a while, they'd moved onto the larger estate and begun a few renovations. They were also expecting their first child at the end of the year.

Creed was happy for them, truly he was, but he had to admit he missed running into his brother in the hall between their two front doors. Or only having to cross that small space in order to talk to him.

His brother's willing ear and sage advice would certainly come in handy at the moment, though he imagined Case's response to Creed's dilemma would be much the same as he'd already concluded on his own.

Stay away from Maya. Chalk up tonight's activities to scratching a long-standing itch, then put it behind him and move on.

Not a problem. He'd pretty much made that decision even before he'd rolled off the bed at Maya's house and made his hasty exit.

And a few shots of scotch could only bolster his determination, he thought, as he let himself into his apartment and headed straight for the liquor cabinet.

Three

The Fortune Estate was about the last place Maya wanted to be right now. But it was Nash's birthday, and even though he'd insisted he didn't want to celebrate—in fact, that he was in no mood to celebrate while his beloved Patricia's whereabouts were still unknown—the Fortune children had been adamant about getting together.

They were keeping the so-called party low-key. No decorations and no guests other than immediate family, just a relaxed cookout and a few understated gifts for the man of the hour.

Maya parked along the side of the wide circular drive at the front of the mammoth, gothic-style stone mansion. The trim light gray with wrought iron accents and a black roof. It sat on a hundred and seventy-five acres about twenty miles west of Sioux Falls, just outside the plush suburb of Colonial Pine Hills.

The main house consisted of seven bedrooms and nine bathrooms, but there was also a pool, guest house, stable and the cottage where Skylar and her new husband, Zack Manning, were living until their baby was born. After that, they planned to move back to New Zealand, where they would work together on the horse breeding venture they both had dreamed of.

The property also boasted a small lake and numerous trails that Maya and the Fortune children had all made great use of when they were younger.

Her shoes crunched on crushed stone as she made her way over the drive, beneath the porte cochere and across the wide verandah to the front door, her gift for Nash clutched in her hands. She was wearing a simple yellow sundress and her hair was pulled back in a French braid.

If it weren't for Nash, she wouldn't be here at all. Being around the Fortune siblings made her uncomfortable enough under normal circumstances, but it had been only a week since her ill-fated decision to give herself to Creed, and she had no desire to see him again so soon. Or ever, if she could have managed it.

But the only thing worse than seeing him again was letting him think her a coward, and that's exactly what would happen if she begged off attending Nash's party.

Taking a deep breath, she squeezed the latch on the front door and let herself into the large marble foyer with its grand, double staircase and giant chandelier twinkling overhead.

Everything about the Fortune Estate was both comforting and daunting. She'd grown up in this house, so she felt a certain connection and warmth, yet she'd also always felt out of place within the family, and suffered a sense of detachment whenever she found herself once again inside the vast, artfully decorated walls.

That was part of the reason she didn't return home very often, and hadn't since she'd left for college.

The other part was her deep-seated reluctance to run into Creed.

She laughed silently to herself, the mocking sound reverberating through her brain. How ironic that she'd spent years avoiding the man as often as she could, only to find herself even more desperate to do so now that they'd slept together.

The front of the house was empty, but she heard voices coming from the back and knew everyone was already gathered out on the west verandah, overlooking the pool.

She moved to the right through the cavernous foyer and west gallery area to the hallway leading past the dining and gathering rooms.

Most of the house was decorated in shades of pale gold and deep red—her mother's choice when she'd redone the interior of the estate soon after marrying Nash. The kids, including Maya, had of course been allowed to decorate their own private living quarters when they'd gotten old enough.

The Fortunes also boasted an impressive collection of modern art and sculpture, some of it lovely, some slightly obscure. For the most part, Nash and Patricia added pieces that caught their fancy, and for no other reason.

Above all, the one thing that could be said for the house—which could have easily come across as showy and pretentious—was that regardless of the extravagant decor, it was comfortably livable.

The closer she got to the verandah, the louder the voices grew. There was laughter and merriment, but it was more subdued than usual. No matter what they were doing or what the conversation might be, there was no denying that Patricia's absence was foremost on everyone's mind, weighing down their hearts.

Maya wished, not for the first time, that there was something she could share, some snippet of information she knew or remembered that would help to find her mother. But no matter how hard she concentrated, nothing came to mind.

Standing in the doorway leading outside, she observed the entire Fortune clan in action.

Nash and the women of the family were seated at a large round patio table. The two Fortune daughters, Eliza and Skylar, sat closest to their father. Case's wife, Gina, Blake's fiancée, Sasha, and Max's wife, Diana— the two were back in town—made up the rest of the circle, with empty chairs in between for the missing men. They sipped lemonade from tall, hand-painted glasses and munched on potato chips and an assortment of vegetables surrounding a large bowl of dip.

A couple of servants bustled around them unobtrusively, topping off drinks, making sure the platters of food never emptied and providing anything else the family might need.

Across the verandah, at a shiny silver gas grill the size of a small car, Case, Blake, the Australian cousin, Max, Eliza's husband, Reese, and Skylar's New Zealander husband, Zack, stood together. The men were holding frosted mugs of frothy, imported beer and arguing good-naturedly about how well-done the steaks sizzling on the hot rack should be.

And, of course, there was Creed. He stood out from the rest, seeming taller, darker, more handsome. He was also the one manning the grill, holding the others at bay with a long metal spatula that he wielded like a sword before turning to flip the big chunks of browning meat.

Maya's stomach tightened at the sight and at the memories that flooded her of their single night together.

Creed, she was sure, would be plagued by no such thoughts or memories. He was over her, remember? Now that he'd had her, she was out of his system.

That's what he'd said, his parting shot as he'd turned and walked out of her bedroom, out of her house.

Too bad he hadn't also walked out of her life. She wouldn't be standing here, struggling for breath and feeling like she might throw up, if he had.

She didn't know which was worse—having to attend a Fortune family gathering when she wasn't a part of the family…or having to face Creed so soon after her intimate humiliation at his hands.

Without her mother there to make her feel more at ease, she almost wanted to turn around and leave before anyone noticed her, especially Creed. But she knew how much Patricia loved Nash, and that she wouldn't want him to be unhappy. Maya also knew that her mother would want her to do whatever she could to try to ease Nash's burden.

That meant attending this party, in spite of her personal reservations.

Taking a deep breath, she stepped out onto the verandah with a smile on her face, hoping no one would notice how forced it was.

Nash spotted her first and rose from his place at the table to greet her.

"Maya, sweetheart! You're here."

He hugged her and kissed her cheek, and at least a portion of her grin turned genuine.

"Happy birthday," she told him, handing him the be-ribboned gift, a gold money clip engraved with his initials.

"You didn't have to do that," he said, but the corners of his eyes crinkled with pleasure. He took the present and set it with a pile of other brightly wrapped boxes of varying sizes on a low cedar bench along the outer wall of the house.

"Come sit down," he invited, taking her hand and leading her over to the table. The women smiled in greeting, the men waving and calling out from the other side of the verandah.

Only one person failed to say hello and looked less than pleased by her arrival. From the corner of her eye, she saw Creed's expression tighten, his hard gaze on her as he lifted the mug of beer to his lips and took a long swallow.

He certainly wasn't looking at her like a man who'd recently shared her bed…or wanted to repeat the experience. In fact, she couldn't say he was looking at her any differently than he ever had.

The realization shouldn't have wounded her, but it did, sending an arrow straight through her heart.

Before she could dwell much longer on his indifference toward her, Gina handed her a glass of lemonade and patted the seat of the chair to her left. The sleeveless denim shirt she wore over white shorts completely hid any signs of her pregnancy. Of course, she was only a few months along, still in the first trimester, and they had only just recently shared the news with the family.

Skylar, however, looked ready to pop, even though she still had a couple of months to go before her due date. Once the baby was born and it was safe for them to travel, she and Zach would be going back to New Zealand. They would return to the States to visit, but that's where they planned to make their home.

Maya felt a tiny stab of envy at the picture-perfect lives of the people surrounding her. They were all so happy together, and now positively ecstatic about the impending births of the next generation of Fortunes.

And they deserved it. No doubt about it. But Maya couldn't help the longing and regret that welled up within her when she compared their level of happiness with her own.

She and Nash, it seemed, were the only ones whose lives were in shambles. And at least her stepfather's misery was reasonable and already public, so he didn't have to hide his emotions from everyone. Maya, however, spent the majority of her time pretending to be happier than she was, while inside she felt like weeping.

Sparing a quick glance at Creed, who was busy flipping the steaks again, she decided he didn't belong in the same category as Nash and her. He didn't look miserable in the least, and she was pretty sure he had no interest in settling down anytime soon. Certainly not with her, at any rate.

"Sit down and join us," Gina said with an inviting smile. "I'm so glad you could make it."

"Thank you." Maya took a seat between Nash and Skylar, reaching for a chip and holding on to her glass so she would have something to do with her hands.

"The guys keep saying the steaks will be done soon," Eliza said, her lips twisted wryly. "If you ask me, though, I don't think they know what they're doing. It's been about two hours now, and this rabbit food just isn't cutting it anymore."

Eliza rolled her eyes and flicked a hand over the vegetable tray. "We should have insisted on bringing in caterers or whipping up something a little more civilized, the way we girls wanted, instead of letting the men devise the menu."

"Oh, let them go," Diana said with a light chuckle. "They're enjoying themselves over there, drinking and flexing their muscles. And we can pay them back later when we start talking about babies and nurseries and wedding plans." She cast her gaze around the table at the two expectant mothers and one soon-to-be newlywed.

Skylar waved a hand to hush the discussion. "Shh, shh, here they come."

Maya made a point of not looking at Creed as he set a giant platter of charred meat on the table.

"Steaks are done," he announced. "You can stop your whispering and complaining now."

"We weren't complaining," Eliza responded innocently. "We were just saying how nice it is of you to grill these delicious-looking steaks for us."

Creed shot his sister a pointed look while he took another sip of beer. "Uh-huh."

"I'll get the plates," Sasha announced, jumping up and heading into the house.

"I'll get the potato salad and mixed fruit," Skylar said, starting to rise.

Laying a hand on her arm, Maya signaled for her to stay where she was. "You sit. I'll get them."

The next few minutes buzzed with chatter and movement as items were gathered and the table was set.

When Maya returned to the verandah with a large bowl of mixed seasonal fruit in her hands, she stopped in her tracks to find that the only chair left vacant after everyone had shifted and reorganized the seating to make room for the men was directly beside Creed. She swallowed hard, wishing she could slip back into the house and hide.

Sitting right beside him, so close that their arms and legs would likely brush, was more than she could tolerate.

Unfortunately, it didn't look as though she had much choice.

Forcing her feet to move, she carried the fruit to the table and set it down before circling around to the one lone empty chair and reluctantly taking a seat. She still refused to look at Creed, to even acknowledge his presence, but her skin hummed at his proximity, the hair on her arms standing at attention as if they'd been struck with static electricity.

He flipped a juicy steak onto her plate, but she ignored him. He passed her the bowl of potato salad and refilled her glass of lemonade, but she refused to offer him a word of thanks.

Under the table, his knee bumped into hers, and she went stiff waiting for the contact to end and her lungs to once again resume functioning.

Did he know he'd touched her? Had he done it on purpose, or was it simply a result of the cramped situation? She couldn't be sure.

The conversation through dinner was upbeat, but with an underlying note of gravity, especially any time Patricia's name happened to come up, causing a veil of sadness to fall over Nash's eyes. Whenever that occurred, they all rushed to change the subject and get Nash's mind off the very real concern of his missing wife.

It surprised Maya to see just how much all of the Fortune children cared for their father. What they were willing to do and how far they were willing to go to put a smile on his face and help keep him from wallowing in the sorrow of his wife's absence.

For so long, she'd thought them cold and aloof, but now she realized she may have been mistaken. Maybe her view of them had been skewed by her own internalized feelings of desolation and not fitting in.

Maybe if she hadn't felt so out of place all her life and had opened up a bit more, let the Fortunes truly become her family, she would have seen their warmth and compassion sooner.

She found herself swamped with guilt for that, for not being more open-minded in the past. But she was also glad she was finally beginning to see another side to the people she'd lived with for half her life. It was comforting, lifting her spirits at least for a moment.

She only wished she could identify and alter her feelings for Creed as easily as her feelings for the rest of the Fortunes seemed to be changing. But where he was concerned, her insides were knotted with disillusionment and uncertainty.

He'd come over to her house and made love to her, taken her virginity and then walked out like it meant nothing. She hadn't seen or heard from him since, and now that they were forced to be near each other, he hadn't made a single gesture or remark that even acknowledged what they'd shared.

While her body flushed with heat every time he glanced in her direction or got too close, he was treating her no differently than ever before. Like a sister, not a lover.

She swallowed hard, the last bite of birthday cake she'd just eaten sitting like a lead weight at the bottom of her stomach.

She'd gone from thinking all of her dreams concerning Creed were finally coming true, to having them dashed just as quickly. It was enough to make her want to give up on men altogether.

Glancing surreptitiously at her watch, she decided she'd been at the party long enough that she could make her excuses and slip away.

The meal dishes had already been cleared, Nash had opened his gifts, and everyone had enjoyed at least one slice of cake. And as much fun as she'd had, as glad as she'd been that she could be there for Nash, she didn't know how much longer she could be near Creed without either screaming or bursting into tears.

Using the excuse that she had lessons to correct for school the next day, she quietly made her way around the verandah to say good-night. They all hugged her and kissed her cheek, some asking if she was sure she couldn't stay longer, others inviting her to their respective homes anytime she had a mind to visit.

Maya was touched, and found herself promising she would, even though she had no idea when she would find the time to drive to Deadwood, which was more than three hundred and fifty miles away, let alone fly all the way to Australia.

The only person she didn't bother saying goodbye to was Creed. Although she hadn't done it on purpose, she was able to leave the verandah and head back through the house to her car before he returned from a trip to the kitchen to refill the ice chest with sodas and beer.

That one thing, at least, had fallen in her favor.

Creed caught sight of Maya's retreating form the minute he set foot back out on the verandah with an armful of assorted cans and bottles. It was just like her to sneak away, slink off quietly the same as she had so many times when she was a kid.

He paused for a second until she'd disappeared from view, then strode to the open cooler a few feet away. Dropping the drinks into the pool of melting ice, he slammed the lid closed and turned on his heel.

His brother Case stood nearby, watching his actions with a raised eyebrow.

"Be right back," he said without further explanation, stalking across the verandah and into the house after Maya.

He caught up with her as she was getting into her car. The driver's-side window was down, a soft breeze ruffling the wisps of dark hair that had come loose from her braid to fall around her cheeks and temples.

"Maya, wait up."

For a minute he thought she was going to ignore him and drive away, even though he was sure she'd heard him. Then her shoulders seemed to slump and her hand fell from where it had been ready to turn the key in the ignition.

Slowly she lifted her head to meet his gaze. Her brown eyes, usually so soft, were cold. She didn't say anything, simply stared at him and waited for him to speak.

He wondered if she realized what a beautiful woman she was, then could have kicked himself for letting the thought slide through his mind. She was off-limits, that's all there was to it, and he had no intention of lowering his defenses enough for a repeat of the mistake he'd made last week.

It was true, though. The half-Sioux blood running through her veins made her features striking. High cheekbones, brown eyes and dark, sultry skin all came together to create a stunningly sensual package.

If she stopped wearing the shapeless dresses and oversize tops and slacks she was so fond of, she'd be a real knockout. Of course, then she would have even more men sniffing around her skirts than she already did.

A flash of anger poured through him and his jaw clenched. Whatever he'd planned to say when he'd first followed her out here was suddenly replaced by the image of her with other men, including that Brad McKenzie she'd been seeing for the past year.

His teeth ground together even harder. Creed was the first man she'd been with; he knew that because he'd been the one to take her virginity. And up to now, he'd felt a little guilty about that.

But if her first time hadn't been with him, it probably would have been with McKenzie, and that was somehow an even more bitter pill to swallow.

"Where are you going?" he asked, his voice sharp, with an accusing edge he hadn't intended when he'd approached her.

She bristled visibly, her knuckles going white where she gripped the steering wheel. "Not that it's any of your business, but I have papers to grade before school tomorrow."

At her response, the tension in his muscles began to ease. He didn't know what he'd expected her to say, but he was unaccountably relieved the answer didn't have anything to do with another man. Especially McKenzie.

He leaned down, resting an arm on the roof of the car while his other hand rested on the open window frame of the driver's-side door.

In a tone more relaxed than before, he said, "Just so you know, I hired a couple of extra private detectives to look into your mother's disappearance. Some guys

I've worked with on and off over the years. They're good, so hopefully we'll have some information soon."

Seconds ticked by in silence with her gaze locked on his. Her tongue darted out to lick her dry lips and she nodded. "Thank you."

Pushing away from the car, he straightened and shoved his hands into the front pockets of his jeans. "I did it as much for Dad as for you. The P.I.s he hired don't seem to be making much progress, and I figured a few more men on the job couldn't hurt."

He took a step back and then another, the soles of his boots crunching on the stone drive as he put a safe distance between them. If he didn't, he was afraid he'd be tempted to do something stupid.

Like kiss her again.

And that was a definite no-no, so the sooner he went back inside and let her be on her way, the better.

"Thanks for coming. It meant a lot to Dad. Drive carefully," he added, then spun on his heel and put her promptly out of his mind.

Four

Maya was in the middle of a math lesson when the office buzzed that she had a phone call. Butterflies fluttered wildly in her stomach while she went next door to ask Mrs. Kurschbaum to watch her class for a few minutes. Then she walked down the hall to the teachers' lounge where she could use the phone.

She hoped it wasn't Brad again. He didn't make a habit of calling her at work unless it was important, but lately he'd been more dogged than usual in his attempts to get ahold of her.

Not that she could blame him, since she'd been avoiding him as assiduously as he'd been trying to get in touch with her. She'd spoken to him a few times, but so far managed to circumvent seeing him in person.

She knew he was getting suspicious, that he knew something was wrong or going on behind his back. And he was right, because she simply didn't know how to face him after sleeping with Creed.

She'd been dating Brad for nearly a year, growing closer by the week. She even thought they might have eventually ended up walking down the aisle. Even so, when it came to moving past first or second base, she'd kept him at arm's length.

But the minute Creed looked at her with so much as a hint of passion in his shadowy blue eyes, she'd fallen into bed with him faster than he could say "pretty please."

A rush of shame washed over her at the memory. She'd thought that night was the beginning of happily-ever-after for her, but Creed's behavior immediately after they'd made love had disabused her of that notion quickly enough.

Now she almost felt like an adulteress, as though she'd cheated on Brad with a much less desirable man.

Well, not less desirable. Creed could never be described as that.

Oh, no, he was still infinitely desirable. No matter how hard she tried to deny it or to block him from her heart and mind, she couldn't seem to *stop* being attracted to him.

She wished to heaven she could. It would make her life so much easier.

Finally reaching the teachers' lounge and phone, she lifted the handset and punched the blinking button for line three.

"Hello?"

"Maya?"

It wasn't Brad, and the butterflies in her stomach didn't know whether to settle down or speed up. She swallowed hard and lowered herself into a nearby chair.

"I'm in the middle of a class, Creed. What do you want?"

Was there nowhere she could be safe from of this man? Bad enough she ran into him at the Fortune Estate every time she went to visit. Even those times she did her best to avoid being there when she thought he might be around. But now he was showing up at her house and calling her at work.

She wished she knew where her mother was. Wished Patricia had said something before she'd disappeared, and that Maya might have had the chance to go with her. Anything to gain a little peace from Creed Fortune's overwhelming, overbearing and increasingly painful presence.

"We need to talk," he said without apology for making her abandon her students in the middle of a lesson. "When school lets out, don't leave. I'm going to pick you up."

Her brow creased. "Why?" And then her heart skipped a beat. "Has something happened? Is it my mother? Did you find—"

"I have some information, but we can't discuss it now. I'll pick you up in a couple hours."

Before she could protest or demand he tell her what was going on, the line went dead. She sat in stunned silence for another minute the dial tone ringing in her ears as loudly as Creed's words.

When she thought she could function without feeling as if she'd just run face-first into a lamppost, she returned the phone to its cradle and walked slowly to her classroom. She thanked Mrs. Kurschbaum for watching her students and somehow managed to stumble her way through the rest of the day.

Her mind raced the entire time, her pulse not far behind. She wondered what Creed had found out. Did he know where her mother was? Was she all right?

The end of the day couldn't come quickly enough, and as soon as the kids had gathered their things and raced out of the building, Maya grabbed her purse and followed. Normally she would have stuck around for a while, straightening the room, dealing with paperwork, even gathering a few things to take home with her. Today, though, she left everything behind in her mad dash for the parking lot.

Buses loaded with rambunctious children were pulling away from the curb. She smiled and waved several times as students who weren't used to seeing her again before they went home called her name, but her eyes were scanning the area for Creed's car.

As the last bus lumbered off, she spotted his midnight-blue Mercedes-Benz turning into the school's main drive. He coasted to a stop directly in front of her, the tinted windows hiding everything inside the vehicle from view.

Reaching for the latch, she yanked the door open and jumped inside. She twisted in her seat to face him, slightly out of breath, not from exertion but anxiety.

"All right, what's going on? Did you find Mom?"

He shook his head, keeping his gaze trained straight ahead as the car rolled forward. "Not yet. Let me get you home first."

"Home? Why call me in the middle of the day and pick me up at all when you could have just waited until I got home and met me there? Tell me what's going on, Creed."

He slowed to check traffic, then pulled away from the school and onto the main road.

"Soon. Now buckle up." Reaching across her, he grabbed the seat belt and stretched it toward him, fumbling blindly for the snap while he kept his eyes on the road.

With a frustrated sigh, she took the buckle out of his hand and clicked it into place herself. Although she wanted to argue, she knew better than to think she could get him to say anything before he was darn good and ready.

Thankfully, her town house wasn't far from the school, so it wouldn't take them long to get there. Still, she spent the ten-minute drive tapping her foot, fisting and unfisting her fingers, drumming her nails on the armrest.

She was surprised Creed didn't tell her to cut it out. But then, he seemed preoccupied himself, his jaw set in a tight line, his knuckles white on the steering wheel, more intent on his driving than usual.

When they reached her house, he found a place to park and cut the engine. Throwing open his door, he came around to hers, but she was already out, digging in her purse for her keys.

She unlocked the front door and let them both in, then tossed her purse aside and turned on him.

"Okay," she said, her arms folded beneath her breasts. "We're home. Now tell me what's going on."

He nodded, shrugging out of his jacket and loosening the tie knotted around his neck. He tossed both over the back of a kitchen chair, then headed for the living room.

Rolling her eyes, she clamped down on the urge to scream and followed him. She found him taking a seat on her sofa, his fingers undoing the buttons at his collar and wrists, rolling the stark white material of the dress shirt to his elbows.

"Have a seat," he told her, patting the cushion on his right.

"If I do, I want you to tell me what you found out," she demanded. "No more stalling."

Meeting her gaze for the first time since he'd picked her up at school, his mouth lifted in a half-hearted grin. "Sit down, Maya."

As much as she didn't want to, she stepped forward and lowered herself onto the sofa beside him. She jerked slightly when he laid one of his large hands over hers where it rested on her knee.

"One of the private investigators I hired contacted me this morning with some information about your mother. And I want you to know that I haven't said anything to anyone else yet. Not even Dad. I wanted to talk to you first and thought you should be the first to know."

She frowned, her concern growing by leaps and bounds at his soft tone and kind attitude toward her. He wasn't usually this nice, which meant something terrible must be going on.

"Just tell me," she forced herself to say past a throat growing tight with dread.

Lifting her hand from her knee, he turned it over and linked his fingers with hers. At another time the action would have warmed her, made her think that maybe he had feelings for her after all. Now it only made her realize how ominous the news he had to share must be.

"It turns out Patricia isn't actually a widow, as she's always claimed. Her first husband—your father— Wilton Blackstone, is alive. The investigators tracked him down and had a little talk with him. Leaned on him a bit," he said, the slight lift of one dark brow telling her exactly what he meant by "leaned on."

"It turns out he's been blackmailing Patricia for months, threatening to tell Dad that their marriage isn't valid because she's still legally married to him. We think that's why she disappeared, that she ran off to get away from your father—and to keep mine from finding out the truth."

Maya sat in stunned silence, her mind trying desperately to make sense of everything Creed had just told her.

Her father was still alive? Her mother had been lying to her all these years? Lying to Nash and the entire Fortune family?

Tears prickled behind her eyes, and her heart felt as though it would pound out of her chest.

"I don't understand," she said in a watery voice. "How can that be? If my father is still alive, where has he been all these years? Why didn't Mom tell me? And why didn't any of Nash's private investigators discover this earlier?"

"I don't know why Dad's guys didn't find out about this," he answered softly, "but my guys *are* good. That's why I hired them. I only wish I'd done it sooner. And I don't know why your mother didn't tell you any of this, but according to my sources, for the past almost twenty years, Wilton Blackstone has been living in Texas. I have to tell you, too, that from the sound of it, he's *not* a nice man, Maya."

His free hand moved to her back to rub reassuringly up and down her spine. "What, if anything, did your mother tell you about your father?"

She shook her head, as much to dispel the confusing thoughts and memories swimming around in her brain as to answer his question.

"She told me he was dead, the same as she told everyone else. I was only five years old when…well, when Mom told me he'd died, so I don't remember much about him. And what I do remember isn't good. He was very violent and abusive. Like you said, *not* a nice man."

"I'm sorry."

Overwhelming emotion threatened again, and she sniffed to hold back tears. "It doesn't matter. I don't even know him, and he obviously never cared much about finding or getting to know me if he's been alive all these years. I'm worried about my mother. Where could she be if she's hiding from him? She must be so frightened, and she's all alone."

Creed leaned in and pressed a kiss to her temple. His lips were warm, even through her hair, and she felt an unreasonable degree of comfort despite the common sense telling her it was merely a brotherly gesture and meant nothing otherwise.

"Do you have any idea where she might have gone?" he asked.

Pulling back, she glared at him through narrowed, damp eyes. "If I did, don't you think I would have said something by now? I'm just as worried about her as everyone else and want to find her just as much. Maybe more."

"I know." His fingers trailed up the line of her back and beneath the fall of her hair. Reaching her neck, he began to gently knead her nape. "But now that you understand why she disappeared, I thought something might come to mind, something you wouldn't have thought to consider before. Did your mother ever talk about Wilton, about her habits or behavior when she was with him? What she did when he—" he cringed "—beat her?"

She considered for a moment, but couldn't recall anything that might be helpful. "No, I'm sorry."

He tugged her close, his arm wrapping around her waist and holding her tight against his side. "It's all right. We're going to find her. The investigators are still on the job, and after turning up this information, I'm sure they'll be able to track her down."

"I'm so worried about her," Maya said in a small voice, leaning into him and letting his soothing disposition seep into her bones.

"So am I. But everything's going to be okay. I promise."

Raising her head, she offered him a tremulous smile. He couldn't promise any such thing, and they both knew it, but the words brought a modicum of solace all the same.

"Thank you, Creed. Thank you for being here and for doing so much to try to find my Mom."

His mouth curved slightly, his hands cupping her face as he wiped the tears from her cheeks with his thumbs. "We're all concerned about Patricia. Besides, you're family."

When she met his gaze, she noticed his smile slipping at the edges, and the look in his eyes was anything but familiar.

A spark of awareness flared low in her belly, spreading quickly outward, even as her mind warned her not to be drawn in by his kind words or the heat in his eyes. She'd wandered down that path once before and gotten nothing but heartache for her troubles.

But the heat of his palms caressed her skin, and his blue eyes were as deep and fathomless ·as the ocean during a storm. Pulling her in, making her feel safe.

For months now, she'd felt so isolated and alone. Even with all of the Fortunes rallying around Nash—and thereby remaining in close proximity to her—she'd still felt as though she was all by herself in this situation. No one could truly understand what she was going through.

Nash loved Patricia. She knew that. And in their own way, the Fortune children did, too.

But Patricia was *her* mother, giving them a bond unlike any other. Nobody knew what they'd been through together or what Maya had been going through since her mother had gone missing. The fear, the uncertainty, the insecurity of belonging nowhere and with no one, since Patricia was her only real link to the Fortunes, her so-called family.

She knew it was crazy, foolish and possibly even sheer desperation on her part, but Creed made her feel less alone, more like she belonged, and more as though everything really would work out in the end.

His fingers slid through her hair to cup the back of her skull and tilt her face up to his. She closed her eyes and surrendered to what she was beginning to consider the inevitable.

He was her Achilles' heel, her weakness. When he was around, her insides turned to mush and her brain ceased to function.

They'd done this before. She'd capitulated before.

Capitulated? More like thrown herself into his arms wholeheartedly and had practically been planning the wedding before the sheets were cold.

And immediately afterward, he'd gotten dressed and walked away.

That's why she was crazy to be letting this happen again. She knew better. She knew he would only hurt her—again.

The minute his mouth touched hers, the insanity seemed more than worth the price of admission. His lips were warm and firm, tasting of coffee and something else she couldn't quite identify. Maybe it was simply Creed, his unique essence invading her every pore.

His arms snaked around her back, holding her, cradling her against his hard chest. Her own arms felt leaden as she lifted them to his shoulders and neck, moaning as he deepened the kiss.

He'd said she was out of his system, that once he'd had her, he could move on. But this was far from moving on. He was just as involved in the kiss as she was, just as eager for more, and that gave her a sense of power she'd never experienced before.

Despite his claims to the contrary, he wanted her as much as she wanted him. Maybe not forever, or for more than this very moment, but it was enough.

She threaded her fingers through his hair, holding him closer and urging him on. His own hands began to tug at the tail of her shirt, tucked into the waistband of charcoal-gray slacks.

When he had the material free, he spanned her bare waist with his warm, broad hands. His fingertips were like conductors, sending tiny shockwaves through her, everywhere they touched.

Her limbs felt heavy, almost immovable. Heat pooled low in her belly, making her squirm with wanting, with need, with eagerness. The emotions rolled up her throat and came out her mouth, where it was still clamped tight to his. He groaned back and delved even more deeply with his tongue.

His hands beneath her blouse slid higher, skimming the edges of her modest white bra, then the undersides of her breasts and her quickly beading nipples within the cotton and lace. At the clear signs of her physical response to his caresses, he grew bolder, reaching around to release the hooks at the center of her back.

With the garment hanging loose around her, he was able to slide his hands up and under. He cupped her firmly in both palms, his thumbs alternately flicking and then drawing circles around the puckered centers.

She was writhing now, desperate for everything he could give her. One of her pumps slipped off her foot and fell to the floor with a clunk as she tried to crawl farther onto his lap. He grabbed her thigh and pulled her closer, brushing stray wisps of hair away from her neck so he could brush his lips over the rapidly beating pulse point.

Her fingers fumbled between them, working to release the row of buttons at the front of his dress shirt. With her head tipped back and her eyes closed in ecstasy, it was a simple task turned almost impossible.

But Creed took mercy on her, undoing the even smaller buttons on her blouse before finishing his own.

As soon as the two sides of the soft cotton separated, she drove her fingers under the collar and into the arm holes, pushing it down his strong, well-muscled arms. The cuffs caught at his wrists and she gave a small cry of frustration.

He chuckled and yanked back while she still held the edges of material in her clenched hands. Fabric tore and she heard buttons ping across the room.

His broad chest was gloriously bare as he sat back, studying her through heavy-lidded, desire-darkened eyes.

"Your turn," he whispered.

Not waiting for her to protest or comply, he reached out to strip both blouse and bra from her upper body.

The cool air of the room washed over her heated skin, making her shiver, and she suddenly felt self-conscious of her nudity.

They'd done this once before. She'd already been naked in front of him, but she wasn't quite ready to sit on her couch, in broad daylight, with her breasts hanging out.

She lifted her arms to cover herself, but Creed

stopped her, wrapping his fingers around her wrists and holding them away.

"Don't," he warned in a low voice. "You're beautiful. You should be proud of your body instead of hiding inside those oversize dresses and loose pantsuits you like so much."

His hands slid from her wrists to her elbows, then back, making the little hairs on her arms stand on end. She shivered again, even though she was far from cold this time.

And she squirmed, because his words made her uncomfortable. She wasn't beautiful; she knew that. She was plain and rather average looking.

But for this one moment in time, he made her *feel* beautiful. Sexy and sensual, even. His gaze, glittering with barely restrained passion, skimmed over her, singeing her from head to toe as thoroughly as an open flame.

He brought her hands to his mouth, one after the other. Pressed his lips to each of her knuckles in turn, then the center of her palms and the tiny, bluish veins on the insides of her wrists.

Any vestiges of shyness disappeared beneath his tender assault and reignited her yearning a thousand percent. Physiologically impossible or not, she felt ready to melt like an ice cube left too long in the sun.

He placed her hands, with their now-tingling digits, on his bare shoulders before leaning in to press a soft kiss to the corner of her mouth. He followed that up with a kiss to the other corner, then her cheeks, temples, eyelids.

While his lips drifted softly over her face, his hands toyed briefly at her breasts on their way to her waist, where he made quick work of loosening her slacks and pushing them down her hips. She moved in whatever ways he needed to get the pants, pantyhose and her underwear all the way off.

As soon as that was done, he shed his own shoes and expensively tailored dress pants, leaving everything in a wrinkled pile on the living room floor. All she could do while this was going on was knead his shoulders and squirm with the longing pumping through her veins.

Reality prodded the outer edges of her mind, threatening to ruin the cloud of euphoria that had formed around them, but she wouldn't let it. Tomorrow would be soon enough to deal with the fact that this wasn't real and wouldn't last. Soon enough to go back to the near-hostile stepsibling relationship that kept them walking on eggshells around each other.

Today, this very moment, she had a second chance at living out a lifelong fantasy, and she had every intention of taking full advantage of the opportunity.

Five

Grasping Maya under the arms, Creed scooped her up and redeposited her on the couch. He wanted her under him, open to him and arranged in such a way that he didn't have to worry about dropping her or bouncing her off the sofa at some highly inopportune moment.

Reaching blindly toward the floor, he groped for his pants and fumbled around until he found a condom tucked safely in the folds of his wallet. He kept one there at all times, just in case, and thanked God he'd remembered to add another packet after the first night he'd spent with Maya.

Keeping his gaze locked on her—her flushed face,

the rapid rise and fall of her bare, lovely breasts—he tore open the plastic square and safely covered himself.

Then, with her back against the arm at one end of the sofa and the soft, wide cushions supporting her lithe, blessedly naked form, he spread her legs and settled himself firmly between them. If he had a choice, he would keep her like this forever and never move out of the cradle of her smooth, welcoming thighs.

He should have left twenty minutes ago. Should have called her at school, or even waited until she'd gotten home, to tell her what the private investigator had found out about her mother and not-dead-after-all father. It would have been the safer route to take.

But he hadn't been able to bring himself to break news like that over the phone. And the twenty-minutes-ago ship had clearly sailed. Hell, the vessel was halfway around the world by now. He couldn't leave her now if someone held a gun to his head.

Lapse in judgment or not, he'd started this and he was damn well going to finish it.

Not that making love to her again was going to be any great trial. He was already so hard for her, he was ready to burst.

Their bodies melded together from chest to pelvis, his erection straining toward her warm, damp center. But he wasn't ready to end this encounter quite so quickly. He wanted to make it last, wanted the swirling, ragged sensations building inside them both to linger a while longer.

He kissed her, brushing her lips and teasing her tongue with only a fraction of the passion burning in his gut. His fingers sifted through her long, silky hair, spreading it out around her head, like a dark cloud in a thunder-riddled sky.

Abandoning her mouth, he trailed a line of nips and licks down her throat to her breasts. She was clawing at his shoulders, upper arms, and whatever part of his back she could reach. Driving him crazy and straining his already tenuous control.

He thought about grabbing her wrists again to keep her from sending him straight over the edge, but what she was doing felt too damn good. So he started counting from one to ten and back again—slowly, in three languages. Mentally reciting a few statistics for local sporting teams that came readily to mind. Re-hashing the details of a recent business deal he and Case had made for Dakota Fortune. Anything to keep the top of his head from shooting off before he'd even gotten to the best part of being naked with Maya Black-stone.

And if she was going to take him to the brink, almost without trying, then he fully intended to do the same to her.

He began to feast at her breasts as he'd always dreamed, taking his time and being thorough. He circled one of the swollen peaks with the tip of his tongue, then scraped the rough surface across the pointed nipple. At the same time, he teased the other breast, squeezing, rubbing, tweaking with thumb and index finger. She squirmed beneath him, arching her back and offering herself to him more fully.

"Creed, please."

Her voice was a whimper, and a streak of power rushed through him. She was his for the taking. At his mercy. He could do just about anything to her and she wouldn't try to stop him.

But he didn't want to do anything *to* her, he wanted to do it *with* her. Now.

Without abandoning her breasts completely, he slid a palm down the plane of her stomach, into the triangle of springy curls between her legs to test her readiness. She was hot and wet against his fingers, and he groaned, clamping his jaw to keep even more desperate, pathetic sounds from working their way up his throat.

"I'm going to take you now," he all but growled.

A warning or a promise, he wasn't sure. He worked two fingers gently into her channel and was rewarded by the jerk of her hips and a high mewling rolling past her lips.

"Yes, please," she panted when she was capable of speech. "You're taking too long as it is."

He started to chuckle but ended with a low moan as she brought her legs around his waist and locked them at the ankles.

"Hey," he grated, surprised his brain was still functioning well enough to send sensible signals to his vocal chords. "Who's the more experienced person here? How would you know I'm taking too long?"

"I just do. Now get to it already," she demanded.

To emphasize her point, she moved a hand from his bicep to the narrow space between their sweat-slick bodies and wrapped her slim fingers around his burgeoning length.

The action was so shocking, and so pleasurable, he nearly came.

His muscles tensed, his entire frame going rigid as he fought to pull himself back from the point of no return. Inhaling and exhaling carefully, breathing through his nose as though he'd just run a thousand-yard dash, he covered her hand and pried open her surprisingly strong grip.

"Don't do that," he said, moving her hand a safe distance from what he now considered the danger zone.

At his firm reprimand, her chocolate-brown eyes turned cloudy and she seemed to pull back. Not physically, but emotionally. At her side, her fingers curled into a loose fist.

Dammit. Creed cursed himself and then Maya's innocence. She was too inexperienced to know just how close he was to losing it. To not only embarrassing himself, but robbing them both of the ultimate pleasure their joining could bring.

He wasn't used to dealing with virgins. Even if Maya was no longer a technical virgin, she had been only a week ago—before he'd taken her the first time. For all the more she knew about men and sex, she might as well still be one.

"Not because I don't like it," he told her, quickly trying to repair any damage he might have caused. "Believe me, I do. Too much. But if you keep touching me that way, I won't last long enough to get inside you. And I very much want to be inside you."

He watched the tendons of her throat tighten and release as she swallowed.

"So…I can touch you later?" she asked, her tone tentative.

He gritted his teeth even harder to stifle a groan, his fingers flexing on her hips. "Yes, you can touch me later. Touch me, kiss me, do whatever you like to me." He shuddered as his mind filled with visions of her taking him into her mouth. "Later."

She nodded, her expression solemn. "All right."

A second later she wiggled beneath him, her legs squeezing around his waist, her hands curling over his shoulders and drawing him closer.

"Hurry up and come inside me, then, so I can hurry up and touch you however I want." She smiled wickedly, her tongue darting out to lick her lips like a practiced courtesan. "I have ideas, and things I've been fantasizing about for years."

His body bucked at her blatant carnal promise, and he marveled that he hadn't burst into flames already.

"Heaven help me," he muttered raggedly. "You'll be the death of me. I won't make it through the hour."

She canted her hips, bringing her feminine center flush with his throbbing groin. "You never know unless you try."

His breath hissed out in a gust. "Devil woman." And then he took her mouth in a passionate kiss, guiding himself into her warm sheath.

Maya gasped as he entered her completely, filling her to the hilt.

She might not be as experienced as Creed, but a girl could definitely get used to this sort of thing: being in the arms of the man she'd had a crush on the majority of her life; having him touch her, kiss her, work her into a frenzy of lust so strong she wanted to weep.

He pounded against her, being less than gentle, but she didn't care. She raised her legs even higher around his waist, allowing him to enter her just a fraction more, until she swore he touched her womb.

Her arms clutched his back, her belly quivering with every stroke of his velvet hardness inside her. She panted for more and whispered in his ear for him to go deeper, faster.

He complied, a muscle in his jaw ticking rhythmically as he gripped her thighs, held her in place, brought her roughly into contact with him on each downward slide.

"Yes." Her lungs burned as she struggled for air. "Please, yes."

"Yes," he agreed, the word slipping from between clenched teeth.

A second later she was flying. Creed's hands and mouth and body worked as a single unit to drive her over the edge, gasping as wave after wave of orgasm shook her to her core.

Following her into the abyss, he ground against her one last time before shouting his release. He sank down on top of her, his heavy weight pinning her in place as their chests rose and fell in a synchronized bid for oxygen.

By the time either of them had the strength to move, the sky outside the town house windows was starting to grow dim with the first pale streaks of dusk. Creed rolled to his side, still holding her as best he could on the narrow sofa. The side of one thumb drew nonsensical designs on her upper arm while the fingers of his other hand drifted through the ends of her hair.

Her eyes were growing heavy, and she thought that if she let them close, she could probably sleep for a week. But he'd promised her something, and she didn't intend to drift off until she was sure he would follow through on their agreement.

She turned slightly, snuggling closer, rubbing her cheek against the smooth skin at the hollow of his shoulder.

"Now that that's done," she said, struggling to keep her tone level and detached, "it's my turn, right?"

Her fingers wandered over his left pectoral, lightly covered with a dusting of dark hair, then lower, down the center of his flat stomach. She felt his abdominal muscles tense as he sucked in his breath.

"Your turn for what?" he asked.

With her head tipped away from him, he couldn't see

her smile. He wasn't fooling her, though. Regardless of his words, his body knew exactly what she was talking about.

She lifted her face to his, leaning in to catch his bottom lip gently between her teeth and give it a little tug. "To touch you. Anywhere I like. Any way I like. Remember?"

He opened his mouth to deny it, even started to shake his head. But when she took hold of his reviving member and gave it a little squeeze, he could only groan in surrender.

"All right, all right. Yes, I remember. But are you sure…?"

She pumped him again, just once, but with enough pressure to let him know she meant business. He moaned again, a low, ragged sound, and closed his eyes as his head fell back against the arm of the couch.

Grinning at his acquiescence and the sudden rush of power bubbling through her bloodstream, she shifted around to straddle his legs and hover above him.

It was going to be a long night, and she intended to enjoy every minute of it to the absolute fullest.

And if she had her way, she would make sure Creed did, too.

Creed lay in the dark of Maya's quiet bedroom, wide awake and kicking himself for what he'd done. He'd let down his guard and touched her a second time when he never should have touched her the first time.

Second time, hell. Try third, fourth and maybe fifth times; he'd lost count somewhere around midnight.

For only recently losing her virginity, she'd been insatiable. Not that he'd tried very hard to put her off or keep himself from turning to her over and over again.

He never should have touched her to begin with. He knew that. But now that he had, he couldn't seem to stop. She was a fire in his blood, and he seemed powerless to stay away from her.

He sighed, then went rigid when she burrowed closer to his side. They'd already made love multiple times. So often and with such enthusiasm that Maya had finally fallen into an exhausted sleep.

But try telling that to his libido. The feel of her soft curves nestled against him like a second skin brought his arousal flaring back to life.

Her head on his shoulder…her silky hair falling across his arm…her dainty hand curled on his chest… one leg drawn up and twined with his own. How could any man resist such an enticing temptation, regardless of the risks involved?

It didn't sit well with Creed to concede that he was as weak as any other male of his species when it came to Maya Blackstone. But part of that weakness, he admitted, stemmed from the fact that she needed him right now.

She had been stunned by the news that her biological father was still alive, and terrified for her mother's safety, especially being aware that Wilton Blackstone was likely the reason for Patricia's disappearance. He'd seen the shock and despair etched clearly on her face as he'd broken the news.

That's why she'd turned to him, and why he'd allowed himself to move past the invisible barriers he'd erected to keep her at arm's length.

She'd needed him. Needed comfort and human contact, the distraction of physical intimacy to get her mind off the situation with her mother. And, God help him, he hadn't been able to walk away from her, even if he'd wanted to.

He tipped his head to stare down at her, doing his best not to notice the generous swell of her breasts or the way they spilled so attractively across his chest.

She still needed him, and would until her mother was found and brought home where she belonged. As soon as that happened, all of their lives would go back to normal and he would be able to leave her alone, focus his mind—and hormones—on other things.

Stress and uncertainty, that's all this was. They were both acting completely out of character, and he felt the tightness in his lungs and diaphragm ease at that crystal-clear realization.

As long as what was going on between them at the moment remained private, and no one—especially the media—found out, they would be okay.

He swallowed, relaxing more fully into the pillows at his back. Beside him, Maya stirred. Her soft brown eyes blinked open and she stretched like a contented cat, her rosy, well-kissed lips curving in a smile when she found him awake and watching her.

"Hi," she said, her voice a sensual purr.

"Hi," he returned with a suggestive grin of his own, welcoming the hot, heavy flush of arousal beginning to pump once again through every cell of his being.

"What time is it?"

He cast his gaze over her shoulder, in the direction of the digital clock on the bedside table. "About 4:00 a.m."

She groaned, closing her eyes and burying her face in his chest. But just as quickly, she came back up, shaking her hair out of the way and starting to press light kisses along the line of his jaw, which he was sure needed a shave by now.

"I have to start getting ready for work in a couple hours," she told him.

"Me, too," he said, bringing his hands up to skim her waist and the small of her back.

"I'll be so tired tomorrow I'll probably fall asleep at my desk."

He gave a rueful chuckle, picturing that very situation and how much ribbing he would get from everyone in the Dakota Fortune offices if they found out about it. "Me, too."

"But that gives us two hours to enjoy ourselves again."

He glanced at the clock, did the math, weighed the pros and cons of missing out on a full night of sleep.

There was no contest—making love to Maya would win every time.

Capturing her mouth, he kissed her breathless, then rolled until he loomed over her, and made sure neither of them got a wink of sleep before the sun broke over the horizon.

Maya had expected to be exhausted all day, but instead she was brimming with energy and couldn't seem to wipe the smile from her face. Not even when Mikey Roth put gum in Sally Mattea's hair, and the little girl screamed bloody murder for almost an hour.

She'd punished Mikey by putting him on animal-clean-up duty for the rest of the week, which basically meant he would be helping her care for the guinea pig and small aquarium of fish she kept as unofficial class-room mascots. Then she'd sent to the cafeteria for some butter and ice cubes, and spent all of recess sitting cross-legged at the edge of the playground, working a giant hunk of watermelon-flavored bubblegum out of Sally's blond, baby-fine hair.

There was no doubt what had put her in such a good mood—a night of mind-blowing sex with the man she'd dreamed of as Mr. Right for half her life.

She knew it was dangerous to let herself get too swept away by what was happening between them. There was no way it would last. No happily-ever-after for her where Creed was concerned.

Frankly, she was surprised he'd stayed with her all

night instead of running for the door as soon as they'd finished their impromptu lovemaking session on the living room sofa.

But he hadn't. He'd stuck around until morning, and they'd definitely made good use of the time.

She couldn't let it go to her head, though. She had to keep her feet firmly on the ground and her heart deeply rooted in reality.

Whatever was going on between the two of them right now was only temporary. Explosive, earth-shattering, beyond her wildest fantasies…but temporary.

Still, they weren't hurting anyone. As long as she kept her wits about her and didn't start imagining that things could develop into more than was possible, she would be all right.

She'd spent the morning carefully considering every angle of the situation, playing out every probable scenario. The result was that she'd decided to move cautiously forward with…whatever this was.

Before Creed had dropped her off at school on his own way back home and to work—because her car was still in the school parking lot from when he'd picked her up the afternoon before—he'd run a hand through her loose hair and leaned across the seats to press a light kiss to her lips. He'd asked her to give him a couple of days to put out more feelers about her mother, see what else his investigators could turn up, and promised that they *would* find her.

She'd nodded, swallowing hard as her fears for

Patricia's safety and emotional well-being came flooding back.

With all the tension and animosity that had passed between Creed and herself over the years, she was amazed at how easy it was to put her faith in him. Their relationship might be shaky, as wispy thin as morning dew, but where her mother's disappearance was concerned, she trusted him implicitly.

Then he'd done something that had shocked her even more than his spending the night with her. He'd told her he was coming over with dinner for both of them after work.

She'd been too flustered and—yes, she admitted it— delighted to question why he didn't want to eat out at a restaurant, in public with her, or why he didn't invite her to his place. That he wanted to see her again was enough. See her, spend time with her, and if the look in his eyes at that moment was any indication, likely spend the night with her again, too.

For as long as it lasted, she would take him however she could get him.

Just the thought made her stomach do somersaults. She put a hand low on her belly in an attempt to still the internal acrobatics while she finished saying goodbye to her students as they gathered their books, jackets and lunchboxes, and raced for the buses outside the building waiting to take them home.

After seeing them off and straightening her desk, she grabbed her own purse and a few papers she *should* look over for the next day's lessons, even though she suspected she wouldn't, and headed for her car.

Only a few more hours before she would see Creed again. Before he walked into her house with an armful of take-out and settled in for a quiet dinner.

He hadn't asked her what she wanted to eat, and she hadn't volunteered the information. But being forced to endure a meal she didn't care for would be a small price to pay for the satisfaction of being with Creed again. Even for just a short time.

Six

For the tenth time in an hour, Creed checked his watch, cursing at how slowly the minutes seemed to tick by. He hadn't done a lick of Dakota Fortune business all day, concentrating instead on uncovering anything else he could about Patricia's whereabouts. Making phone calls, putting a couple more investigators on the case, following a few of his own leads and researching some of the information he already had.

But through it all, in the back of his mind he'd been thinking about Maya and anticipating the hour when he could leave the office without arousing suspicion and head over to see her. Of course, he had a few errands to run on the way.

Dinner. He'd offered to bring dinner over to her place.

He shook his head, confused and uncomfortable with how he found himself continually responding to her.

The plain truth was he wanted to be with her. Their time together was limited, and deep in his gut he felt this urgency to store up as much of her as he could. When he had to walk away—and it would happen sooner rather than later—he wanted to have part of her deep under his skin to get him through the many long, lonely nights ahead.

That's why he'd suggested dinner at her house. He couldn't very well take her out to a fancy restaurant, where anyone might see them together. Especially since he knew he was likely to be looking at her half the night as though he wanted to rip her clothes off.

Ninety percent of the restaurant's patrons might not think anything of it, but it would only take the remaining ten percent—one person familiar with the Fortune family, one reporter, one gossip columnist—to create the very scandal he was trying so desperately to avoid.

He didn't want her to be seen going in or out of his apartment, either, for the very same reasons. Even though he lived on the top floor of the Dakota Fortune building, and her presence there might be accepted during business hours, after hours was a whole different story.

Going to her place seemed the obvious choice. From there it had been a short jump to offering to bring dinner.

Another glance at his watch showed only thirty more minutes until he could safely sneak out and get on with what had been consuming his thoughts all day.

Pushing back from his desk, he stood, scooped up a couple of files he needed to drop off at his brother's office, and headed for the door. He informed his assistant that he probably wouldn't be back before morning, then walked a short distance down the hall.

"Mr. Fortune." Case's assistant greeted him with a smile.

He inclined his head in reply. "Debra. Is it all right if I go in, or is he busy?"

"He just got off the phone, so it should be all right, but let me announce you."

Creed let her, preferring to give Case fair warning of his arrival. The last time he'd walked into his brother's office unannounced, it had been to find Case and Gina entwined like weeds on top of the desk, doing something Creed would have preferred never to witness. He loved his brother and new sister-in-law as much as anyone, but there were some things about their relationship he just didn't need to know firsthand.

He'd backed silently out of the office and never mentioned the incident to Case, but from that point on, he'd made sure to let Debra announce him or knock himself and wait for his brother to give him the all-clear.

Rising from her chair, Debra crossed to a door identical to Creed's own, with a brass name plate labeling it the office of one of the copresidents of Dakota

Fortune, and tapped softly, waiting for Case's muffled response. That she didn't simply open the door and walk right in made Creed wonder if she'd stumbled into an intimate moment or two between Case and Gina herself.

"Your brother is here to see you," she informed Case in a bright, casual tone, leaning around the now-open door.

"Good," Creed heard his brother say, punctuated by what sounded like a pen being tossed down. "I could use an excuse not to deal with this report until tomorrow."

Grinning, Creed strolled into his brother's office and took a seat in front of his desk, tossing the files in his hand on top of Case's already cluttered blotter. Behind him, he heard the click of the door as Debra closed it, ensuring the two brothers' privacy.

"I hate to break it to you, brother, but you're going to have more than one report to deal with in the morning."

Case groaned. "Thanks a lot."

"Look," Creed said, getting down to business, "I'm taking off for the night, but I wanted to fill you in on some information I found out about Patricia, and why I think she ran off."

His expression turning serious, Case listened as Creed told him about the extra private investigators he'd hired to look into their stepmother's disappearance and what they'd discovered about Wilton Blackstone still being alive.

When he finished, Case shook his head and swore

beneath his breath. "Dad won't be happy to hear any of that."

"I didn't tell him. And I'd appreciate it if you wouldn't, either. Not yet, anyway. I don't want to get his—or anyone else's—hopes up in case we're wrong about what we think is going on, and Patricia disappeared for some other reason."

Case nodded in understanding.

Creed shifted in his seat, crossing one ankle on the opposite knee and loosening the knot of his tie. "I've still got my guys looking into it, and looking for her."

"Good," Case murmured, his lips pressed into a solemn line. "Let's pray they find her."

Silence filled the room, the minutes ticking by while Creed focused on a spot outside the tall plate glass windows at his brother's back. He felt Case's gaze on him, and knew his brother was waiting to hear what else he had to say.

The problem was, Creed wasn't sure he should reveal the other problem weighing so heavily on his mind. Case was his brother, probably the person he was closest to in the world, but some things weren't meant to be shared with anyone.

"You might as well spit it out," Case said, reading Creed's mind—or maybe just the tight lines he knew marked his face. "Get it off your chest so you can stop sulking about it."

He wasn't sulking, but it sure did seem to occupy a fair chunk of his time these days.

With a sigh, he let his foot fall to the floor and ran splayed hands through his hair, giving the ends a tug for good measure.

"It's about Maya," he said finally.

"Yeah? What about her?"

"I'm sleeping with her."

He blurted it out quickly, like ripping off a bandage, before he could change his mind, then waited for Case's stunned response. He expected wide eyes, a dropped jaw, maybe a few choice expletives as his brother kicked back his chair and stormed around the room.

Instead Case remained perfectly still for one long minute. Then, very slowly, he said, "Okay. How serious is it?"

"Not…serious." Creed shook his head. "It can't be, not with the way things are."

"What things?" Case wanted to know.

Creed gave him a look hot enough to peel paint from the walls. "She's our sister, for God's sake."

"Stepsister," Case corrected, leaning back in his chair and adopting a less poised, more comfortable position. "Stepsister from Dad's third marriage. She's not *technically* related to us. We—*you*—don't share a single drop of blood with her, or a single strand of DNA."

"Does it matter?" Creed snapped, his brows knitting with annoyance. "She's still family. We grew up with her. Hell, she's ten years younger than I am. For that reason alone, I never should have touched her."

"So why did you?"

Leave it to his brother to cut right to the heart of the matter.

He thought about it for a second. No way was he going to tell Case that he'd been watching Maya for years, thinking decidedly *un*brotherly thoughts about her ever since she'd hit puberty.

"I couldn't seem to help myself," he said instead, his insides twisting at the admission.

Case considered that for a minute, rocking back and forth in the soft leather of his executive desk chair.

"So what's the problem?" he asked. "Maya may be younger, but she's a grown woman. If she's as interested as you are, I don't understand why you'd be concerned."

Muttering a low curse, Creed pushed to his feet and began to pace. "Do you know what would happen if word got out that a Fortune son was sleeping with his own stepsister? The press would have a field day. It could ruin the company, not to mention the humiliation it would cause for Dad and Patricia. And the rest of you…no one in the Fortune family would be safe from the gossip and disgrace."

"Do you really think that would happen? You and Maya *aren't* related, no matter how the media might want to spin things. And even if they did their worst, if you're in love with her and the two of you want to be together, you have to know that this family would support you. We've weathered storms before and come out on top. We can do it again."

Creed stopped a few steps from his brother's desk and absorbed what he was saying. It sounded good, exactly what he needed to hear. Exactly what he probably would have told Case if their situations were reversed.

But that didn't make it any easier for him to believe.

"The only thing I would warn you against," his brother went on in a grim tone, "is not to toy with Maya's affections. If you're not serious about her, then you should probably let her go and keep your distance. But if you are…"

Case took a deep breath, his lips quirking slightly. "If you *are* serious about her, and she's the woman you want to spend the rest of your life with, then don't let anything stand in your way."

Creed scowled, not the least bit comforted by his brother's advice. If anything, it set him more on edge, making his stomach clench with the acidic mix of conflicting emotions.

"Trust me on this, little brother," Case continued. "When a man finds the right woman, he has to hang on to her with both hands."

"Are you speaking from experience?" Creed asked, already knowing the answer.

His brother had been almost annoyingly chipper since his marriage to Gina, and it had only gotten worse since he found out he was going to be a father. And while Creed was happy for him, for them both, Case's good mood at the moment only made his own darker.

"Damn right I am," Case said proudly, grinning from ear to ear as he leaned back in his chair, then sent it rocking silently on its springs.

"And if Maya makes you half as happy as Gina makes me, then you'd be an idiot to let her get away. But if you're just using her as a temporary amusement…" He let the words hang in the air for a second, increasing their impact. "Well, I don't need to tell you how hot it will be when you get to Hell."

One of Case's brows lifted pointedly, and he held Creed's gaze until Creed scrubbed a hand over his face and dropped back into one of the chairs in front of his brother's desk.

After a tension-filled pause, Case sat forward in his own chair, leaning his arms on the edge of his desk. "Whatever you decide, Creed, I'll back you one hundred percent. You can count on that."

Blowing out a breath, Creed nodded and pushed to his feet. "Thanks. I don't know if I feel any better about what's going on, but…thanks."

A quick glance at his watch showed it was past time that he could get away with leaving the office and head over to Maya's to start dinner. His talk with Case tempted him to skip the visit altogether, but since the "date" had been his idea, he didn't feel right backing out at the last minute.

"I have to get going," he explained on the way to the door. "Remember not to say anything to Dad or the others about what the investigators turned up. Hopefully we'll find out something more in a few days, but until then I want to keep it all under wraps."

"You've got it. See you tomorrow."

Creed left his brother shuffling papers, muttering about the likelihood of drowning under the pile of reports now flooding his in-box, and made his way to the underground garage of the Dakota Fortune building where his car was parked.

He would stop at the store and pick up what he needed for the evening meal, then he'd head for Maya's house. The very thought made his muscles tense right down to the soles of his feet.

All day he'd been looking forward to seeing her again, *being* with her again. But after talking with his brother, he wasn't sure that was the smartest move on his part.

Case was right—he shouldn't string Maya along. If he wasn't serious about her, he should walk away, leave her alone, put the distance between them again that had been there the past twenty years.

And he wasn't serious about her. Couldn't be. The risks were too great.

Which meant he had to put an end to this...affair, relationship, lapse of judgment and giant mistake. He had to break it off, the sooner the better.

Sliding behind the wheel of his Mercedes, he started the engine and pretended not to feel the ball of dread that slid down his throat and twisted his gut.

PLAY THE Lucky Key Game

and you can get

FREE BOOKS
and FREE GIFTS!

Do You Have the LUCKY KEY?

Scratch the gold areas with a coin. Then check below to see the books and gifts you can get!

YES! I have scratched off the gold areas. Please send me the 2 FREE BOOKS and 2 FREE GIFTS for which I qualify. I understand I am under no obligation to purchase any books, as explained on the back of this card.

320 SDL ELR4   220 SDL ELW5

FIRST NAME   LAST NAME

ADDRESS

APT.#   CITY

www.eHarlequin.com

STATE/PROV.   ZIP/POSTAL CODE

2 free books plus 2 free gifts   1 free book

2 free books   Try Again!

DETACH AND MAIL CARD TODAY!

(S-D-06/07)

© 2002 HARLEQUIN ENTERPRISES LTD. ® and TM are trademarks owned and used by the trademark owner and/or its licensee.

BUSINESS REPLY MAIL

FIRST-CLASS MAIL   PERMIT NO. 717-003   BUFFALO, NY

POSTAGE WILL BE PAID BY ADDRESSEE

SILHOUETTE READER SERVICE
3010 WALDEN AVE
PO BOX 1867
BUFFALO NY 14240-9952

NO POSTAGE
NECESSARY
IF MAILED
IN THE
UNITED STATES

* * *

The minute she heard Creed at the front door, Maya's heart skipped a beat.

She'd spent the past couple of hours lecturing herself to act normal, nonchalant, to not read more into his offer of dinner than there really was. After all, he could merely be feeling sorry for her, given her mother's continued absence and the news he'd delivered yesterday about her father not being deceased as she'd been led to believe.

She didn't want to think that was the case, but had to admit it was a distinct possibility.

He knocked again, and she rushed to let him in, not wanting him to think even for a second that he wasn't entirely welcome.

"Hi," she said, smiling and a little breathless from her race through the house.

He stepped inside, a large paper sack in one arm, but didn't return her smile. Instead his dark eyes barely met hers and lines bracketed his flattened lips. An aura of tension radiated from him in waves.

Her senses immediately went on red alert, her spine going rigid as she braced herself for the worst.

"What is it?" she asked in a hoarse whisper. "Mom… is she…?"

His expression indicated confusion and then just as quickly cleared. "No. God, no. I'm sorry," he said with a shake of his head, "my mind was on something else, something from work. I haven't heard anything else about Patricia yet. I'm sorry if I scared you."

Stale oxygen poured from her lungs in one long exhalation. "Thank goodness."

Creed still looked distracted as he moved ahead of her and walked to the kitchen. She was so relieved that nothing had happened to her mother—that they knew about, anyway—that she ignored his apparent bad mood and simply followed him.

He set the bag on the counter, then shrugged out of his suit jacket and tie. Laying them over the back of one of the four chairs surrounding the small round table, he loosened his collar and rolled up the sleeves of his pale-blue dress shirt before beginning to remove items from the sack.

"What are we having?" she asked. It was hard to tell from the nondescript cartons and containers stamped with the name of an upscale downtown eatery or from the mingled scents wafting from them. All she knew was that it smelled *good*.

"I'm not sure. I told them to throw together a full-course meal with a little of everything."

Instead of a separate container for each dish, the plates the restaurant provided came already arranged, the way they would if they were dining in.

"Want to grab some forks and glasses?" Creed suggested while he popped the lids off, then reached into the bag for a bottle of wine before setting everything else aside.

"Sure." Glad to have something to keep her busy, she turned for the cupboards, returning a moment later with everything they would need.

Handing him a corkscrew for the wine, she folded cloth napkins for each place setting, adding silverware to both. He filled their glasses, then took a seat at the head of the table.

She swallowed, fighting a return of the nerves that had plagued her even before he'd arrived. Having him look at her like that…so intense, so focused…made her feel on display. As though she'd just had one of those dreams where she showed up at work stark naked.

It surprised her that the skittishness hadn't lessened, now that she and Creed were sleeping together. She'd always thought that when two people became intimate with each other they started to feel *more* comfortable together, not less.

But for her the opposite seemed to be true. Making love with him had opened her to a whole new set of insecurities.

She worried that she would do or say the wrong thing and somehow send their relationship back to the way it had been before—with him treating her as either invisible or a nuisance, and her avoiding him as much as possible.

Most of all, though, she found herself on constant alert for the moment when everything would come crashing down around her. It was inevitable, she knew that, but waiting for it to happen, never knowing when the blow might come, made her jittery.

"Have you found out anything more about Mom?" she asked, taking a seat beside him.

He shook his head. "I was on the phone all day, but so far, nothing. They understand the importance of the situation, though, so I do believe they'll find something soon."

"I hope so."

"It smells delicious," she murmured, turning her attention to the meal in front of her.

They ate for a few minutes in silence, then, without warning, he put his utensils down and fixed his gaze on her. Startled by his sudden, intense focus, she froze, sitting back a little as she raised her eyes to his.

"What?" she asked, feeling like the proverbial bug under a microscope.

"Maya."

His voice was low, gentle, and the bottom dropped out of her stomach. Whatever he was about to say, it couldn't be good if he was using that tone on her.

"Oh, God," she said, her chest growing too tight for anything else.

He winced at her response, his hands balling into fists where they rested on the table, on either side of his plate.

"Maya," he said again. "We need to talk."

Seven

This was it, she thought. The shoe she'd been waiting to have fall, the rug she'd been expecting to have yanked out from under her.

He was going to break up with her. Tell her that it had been fun, a temporary diversion, but now it was time for things to return to normal, for them to go back to being nothing more than stepsiblings.

She tried to regulate her breathing, slowly in and out through her nose, but her lungs refused to function properly. Her vision blurred, her mind spinning a mile a minute. He opened his mouth to speak, and she braced for the impact his words would have.

A second later, though, his lips met…parted…met again, as though he was rethinking what he'd been about to say, or trying to come up with the best way to say it.

Shaking his head, he muttered something beneath his breath, too low for her to hear, then picked up his fork and started to eat.

Maya sat in stunned silence. He ate several bites of his dinner, his concentration focused entirely on chewing.

"I've been thinking," he said finally, resting his forearms on the edge of the table and tipping his head slightly in her direction.

Sucking in another breath, she waited, wishing he would just get it over with.

"Maybe we should try looking for Patricia ourselves."

Dammit, that wasn't what he'd meant to say. He'd meant to tell her that going to bed together had been a mistake. That it couldn't happen again and they needed to stay away from each other as much as possible.

"Excuse me?"

His grip on his fork tightened as she stared blankly at him. He couldn't blame her. Tonight wasn't going at all as he'd planned.

He never should have come over, but now that he'd started down this road, he didn't have much choice but to follow through.

Doing his best to act naturally, he resumed eating, but at a slower pace this time.

"You know your mother better than anyone. I'll

keep my investigators on the case, looking into every lead, working to track her down however they can. But maybe it's not such a bad idea for the two of us to take some of their information and go looking ourselves. Two more people out there, pounding the pavement, can't hurt. And if we manage to find her, I can't imagine that your mother would want to see anyone more than she'd want to see you."

It took a full minute for her to digest his words. "All right," she finally responded. "Whatever I can do to help. But…if that was all you were going to suggest, why did you make it sound so dire?"

Without meeting her gaze, he shrugged a shoulder, reaching for his wineglass and taking a long, fortifying sip. "I wasn't sure how you'd feel about taking a few days off work."

It wasn't true, but it sounded good. And what choice did he have now that he'd brought up the idea of trying to track down her mother themselves?

"If you think it will help, and that we actually stand a chance of finding her, of course I'll take a few days. I can call tonight and get tomorrow off, or even the rest of the week if we need it."

He nodded. "I'll call the private investigators in the morning and find out where they think we should start looking first. Wear something comfortable," he added, his lips quirking upward in a small smile. "We could be in for a very long day."

They passed the rest of the meal making only light,

casual conversation. Nothing too deep, nothing too personal. It felt awkward to Maya, but that was a state she was rapidly becoming used to whenever Creed was around.

After they finished eating, he helped her clear the table and put the leftovers in the refrigerator for later. Then he moved to retrieve the wine, holding her glass out to her as he lifted his own to his lips.

"Thank you," she murmured. She took the glass but didn't drink. She'd had two full glasses of the rich pinot noir already. Any more and she was likely to get tipsy.

Tipsy around Creed wasn't good. He already put her too much off balance as it was. Drunk, she'd be lucky if she could string two words together without sounding like a bumbling idiot.

"Dinner was delicious," she said while she still had the capacity to function within normal ranges. "Thank you again for bringing it over."

Rather than answer, he inclined his head. Tossing back the last of his wine, he set the glass onto the counter with a soft clink, then crossed the kitchen to gather his tie and jacket.

"I should get going," he said, slipping the silk tie around his neck but leaving it hanging on either side of his collar, and draping the jacket over his arm.

She placed her own half-full glass beside his, smoothing the palms of her hands down the sides of her skirt as she followed him to the front door.

"I'll swing by around nine o'clock tomorrow to pick

you up. That should give me time to talk to my contacts, get some leads and make arrangements to be out of the office for a couple of days."

"I'll be ready," she said with confidence.

Creed opened the door and took one step out, pausing on the darkened stoop. Only a sliver of moonlight and the occasional porch or streetlamp punctuated the blanket of black that surrounded the neighborhood.

Moving a few inches to the side, she flipped the wall switch for her own porch light so he wouldn't have to walk to the car in total darkness.

"Thank you again." She tucked a strand of hair behind her ear, glancing down at the ground before meeting his eyes once again. "For dinner and hiring the extra private investigators and…everything. It's made this whole situation a little less awful for a while."

In the dim lighting, she couldn't be sure, but she thought he offered a small smile.

"You're welcome."

Stepping forward, he wrapped a hand gently around her arm, just above the elbow, and leaned in. His warm breath danced over her face, and she could smell the musky, attractive scent of his cologne.

"Good night, Maya. Sleep well."

Her lips parted, and she tried to respond. But the minute his mouth brushed her cheek in a soft good-night kiss, every thought in her head dried up like a single drop of water in the midday heat of the Sahara Desert.

Creed straightened, and this time, even in the dark, she could see the blaze in his eyes, the stern set of his jaw.

Her heart lurched, and she felt it all the way to her toes. She licked her suddenly dry lips, her fingers going wide at her sides, as though bracing herself. For what, exactly, she wasn't sure.

His grip on her arm tightened, and then he shook his head, sharply.

"Dammit," he grated, a second before grabbing her other arm, dragging her forward and covering her mouth with his own.

The kiss stole her breath, seared her soul. She could have sworn her lips were burned away, leaving a path of ashes down through the center of her body.

Everywhere he touched, she tingled. From her elbows to her fingertips, where she grasped the sleeves of his jacket. The tips of her breasts that pressed to his chest. The front of her thighs brushing the front of his.

He readjusted the slant of his mouth, giving himself better access and allowing him to deepen the kiss. Their tongues tangled, working them both into a lather of unrepressed need.

Striding forward, he moved into the house again, forcing her to shuffle backward. He kicked the door closed with his foot, the slam reverberating through the room and through her.

But he didn't stop there. Instead he continued

stalking forward, one long, slow step at a time, until she hit the opposite wall.

Spreading his feet on the outside of hers, he pressed his body flush against her own. Flares of heat burst again in her bloodstream, and she wrapped her arms around his neck, bringing them closer.

His hands moved from her arms to her waist, then slid around to cup her buttocks. When he urged her hips up, she went willingly, reveling in the hard ridge of his erection, pressed sharply between her legs.

She was gasping, groaning, and she knew he was with her because he was doing the same. Fisting the hem of her skirt in both hands, he drew the material up, bunching it at her waist. Then he delved beneath and tore her pantyhose and underwear down to her knees.

While he fumbled with his own belt and zipper, she wiggled until she could shed the stockings entirely. As soon as his pants dropped and he reached for her, she was ready, lifting her legs to wrap around his waist.

He slid into her in one slick, smooth glide, making them both gasp at the friction and intense pleasure of finally being linked the way she suspected they'd both been wanting and anticipating all day.

Tugging at the back of his head, she pulled him down for a kiss. Lower, he was moving, stroking, thrusting, pounding into her. She slammed into the wall again and again, but she couldn't have cared less. The wall could take it, and so could she.

Strengthening her grip at both his neck and waist,

she joined him in the powerful, rocking give and take. Only seconds later, she stiffened in climax. Pleasure ripped through her, making her cry out. Her nails dug like talons into his shoulders as she fought desperately to keep her balance and her consciousness.

Inside her, Creed pulsed and thrust one last time before joining her with a shout of completion. Long minutes later she felt his muscles go as lax as her own and let her legs slide weightlessly to the floor.

Clearing her throat, she did her best to get her voice working again. "I'll cook next time," she said just above his ear in barely a whisper. "I was thinking breakfast…if you want to stay the night."

A shudder rolled through him, and he lifted his head to stare down at her. For a beat, his face remained impassive. Then his blue eyes began to sparkle, one corner of his mouth tugging upward in a grin.

"Sounds good to me."

She smiled as he dragged his pants up and fastened the top button, then broke into a full-out laugh when he scooped her up in his arms and headed for the stairs.

"I'm going to want bacon," he told her, the words rumbling through her as she bumped against his chest with each step. "And eggs. Maybe pancakes."

He carried her into the bedroom, tossed her to the middle of the wide mattress and followed her down.

"I can do that," she murmured just as his lips captured hers and he got the blood pumping heavily through her veins all over again.

* * *

Creed lay awake long into the night, chastising himself seven ways from Sunday, while Maya slept at his side, curled so snugly against him they might have shared skin.

He tried to be annoyed, tried to convince himself that she was clinging, that he'd rather be in his own apartment, in his own bed—*alone*—than here with her.

But the truth was, this had all been more his doing than hers. *He'd* been the one unable to resist her soft eyes or the pale, kissable bow of her lips. He'd been the one who couldn't walk away, crossing back over the threshold into her house to take her none too gently against the kitchen wall.

It was everything he shouldn't have done, but he couldn't seem to work up a shred of apology.

Damn, damn, damn. He cursed silently, using a few other, more-creative four-letter words as they came to mind.

This definitely hadn't been part of the plan when he'd knocked on her door this evening. After talking with Case before leaving the Dakota Fortune offices, he'd fully intended to tell her that what had happened between them before couldn't happen again. It had been a lapse, a mistake, the result of a moment—two moments—of weakness, and they had to go back to being only stepbrother and stepsister.

All that and more had been on the tip of his tongue when they sat down to eat. His gut had clenched, but he'd been determined to go through with it, to charge ahead and just get it over with.

And then…he couldn't do it. He'd taken one look in her eyes—at her stricken curious, wary expression, and his throat had gone stone dry.

He was going to burn for it—his brother was right about that—but damned if he could keep his hands off her. The minute his lips had brushed her cheek in what was supposed to be an innocent, brotherly, goodbye peck, he'd known it wasn't enough and had to have more.

Now look where he was. In her bed—*again.* Spending the night—*again.* Making love with her—again and again and again.

He could almost feel the flames of damnation licking at his heels.

But then, it was a hell of a way to go.

Maya shifted at his side in her sleep, and he glanced down, admiring her simple beauty. Her glossy black hair fell over her shoulder and down her back, framing a face any artist would kill to paint, with its high cheekbones and smooth, bronze complexion.

Her body was another work of art, one he'd explored and memorized every inch of it with his eyes, his hands, his mouth…

He didn't want to give that up anytime soon, that was for sure, no matter what his punishment might be later, either in this world or the next.

So maybe it was for the best that he was sticking

around. He wouldn't exactly get an award for Man of the Year, but judging by some of her behavior tonight, she was still very vulnerable where Patricia's disappearance was concerned.

Her panic when he'd first arrived and she'd misread his mood had been enough to convince him she wasn't handling the situation quite as well as she wanted everyone to believe. She was obviously very concerned—as they all were—and petrified that something had happened, or would happen, to her mother before they could find her.

She needed someone right now, and it looked like he was destined to be that person.

He hadn't planned it, he didn't even want it, but that's the way things appeared to be playing out.

For now, he would stick around. He would let things carry on as they had been and hope that nothing hit the fan because of it. If they were careful, no one—Fortune family and the press alike—ever needed to know. And he would deal with the rest later.

After they found Patricia, which he strongly believed they would, he and Maya would go their separate ways, resume their normal lives, never letting anyone so much as suspect that things between them had ventured down a forbidden path.

Hopefully, he wouldn't have any trouble convincing her that it was best for both of them.

Having made that decision, and what peace he could with it for the time being, he pulled the sheet a little higher over them both and closed his eyes, finally sinking into the deep sleep that had eluded him the past few hours.

Maya awoke to kisses being feathered down the side of her neck and over her breasts. It was the most delightful transition into wakefulness she could ever remember experiencing.

Moments later Creed rolled her to her back and wished her good morning in a most improper manner.

Not that she minded. In fact, from the noises she made while he pleasured her from head to toe, it appeared she approved very, very much.

After that, she showered and dressed, then went downstairs to start breakfast while he did the same.

With her hair still damp and left to air dry, she moved around the kitchen, lining an iron skillet with strips of bacon, cracking eggs and mixing batter for pancakes.

She couldn't remember the last time she'd cooked such a large meal. Certainly not for herself. A bowl of cereal or slice of toast and glass of orange juice usually sufficed on her way out the door to work.

But she liked the smells wafting from her stove, enjoyed the task of stirring, beating, turning and making sure that everything cooked properly without burning. By the time Creed came downstairs, dressed in the same suit he'd worn the day before, she was humming and piling two plates with what looked like enough food for an army.

He stopped in the entryway to the kitchen, tightening his tie and smoothing the wrinkles from the sleeves of his suit jacket. She was tempted to offer to iron it for him, but thought that might be a little *too* domestic for whatever was going on between them and wasn't sure he would appreciate the gesture.

"Something smells good," he remarked.

Smiling, she carried the plates to the table and set them down, then proceeded to fill two tall glasses with orange juice.

"Bacon, eggs and pancakes, as requested," she said. When he didn't move, she waved her hand. "Come over here and eat before it gets cold. You did say you wanted to get an early start looking for Patricia, right?"

He nodded, taking a seat in the same spot as he had for dinner the night before. After a few bites he murmured his approval and offered her a small smile.

"This is really good," he told her. "I didn't know you could cook."

She shot him a cockeyed glance, chuckling. "I do have to eat, you know. And I don't enjoy take-out enough to eat it every day."

"Wish I could say the same, but sometimes eating out or ordering in is just easier."

They both cleaned their plates, and this time when Creed helped her clear the table, he let her slip the dishes into the dishwasher for later rather than insisting on doing them by hand.

She knew it was because he wanted to get on the

road and start the search for her mother. He needed to make a few phone calls first, though, to the private investigators he had on her mother's case.

While he used the phone in the kitchen, she wandered around the house, hardly listening to his side of the conversation as she gathered some items she thought they might need. A sweater and her purse, a six-pack of bottled water, fresh fruit and some nutrition bars. She didn't know how long they would be gone or how often they'd be able to stop, and wanted to have at least something on hand to eat and drink.

She'd taken care of the issue of a substitute to cover her classes last night. It had meant calling the woman in charge of those things from her bedside phone, trying to sound sick enough to require time off work while Creed had done his best to make her moan in ecstasy, but she'd gotten her authorization.

If need be, she thought she could even get the whole rest of the week off. She just hoped it wouldn't come to that. She would much rather find her mother right away and be able to bring her home, where she belonged.

Several minutes later he hung up the phone and met her at the front door.

"How did it go?" she asked.

"Good. I have at least a few leads we can follow up on. Places your mother might have used her credit cards and such."

A thrill of anticipation and hope swept through her.

She said a quick prayer that they might actually find her mother today, even though she knew the chances were fairly slim. If Patricia was out there, able to be easily located, then the investigators Nash and Creed had both hired surely would have tracked her down by now.

But there *was* a chance, and she felt better simply taking a more active role in discovering her mother's whereabouts.

Eight

Twelve hours later Maya was exhausted and her optimism was definitely waning.

They'd driven what seemed like thousands of miles, and she was pretty sure they'd crossed the state of South Dakota at least twice in their effort to track down Patricia Fortune.

It was possible her mother had left the state, but since none of Creed's leads specifically led them to believe that was the case, they'd stuck to exploring areas that Patricia could be linked to: the town where Patricia had been born and raised; the reservation where she'd lived with Wilton Blackstone when they were first married, before Patricia had taken a young Maya and run away;

and any number of tiny, out-of-the-way places in between.

Stopping only briefly for lunch and the occasional bathroom break, she and Creed had both gone on almost until they dropped.

She was glad he was driving, because she could barely keep her eyes open. As it was, she found herself raising a hand to cover her yawns every few minutes.

The sun had long since set, and the city of Sioux Falls was lit up with colorful neon signs and the intermittent lights of tall office buildings where some people were obviously working overtime. Traffic was thankfully thin, and except for a few red lights, they were able to skirt the deepest parts of downtown on the way to her town house.

Creed pulled up to the curb, leaving the engine running as he turned to face her. He looked just as tired as she felt, his eyes heavy, the lines of his face deeper than when they'd started out that morning.

"I think it would be best if I spent the night at my place," he said, his voice gritty with fatigue. "I need a long, hot shower and change of clothes before we start out again tomorrow. Will you be all right by yourself?"

She unlatched her safety belt and unlocked the passenger-side door. "Of course. We could both use a good night's sleep."

He glanced down, grimacing at the expensive Italian suit that was now more wrinkled than a Shar-Pei puppy. "Yeah, I'll wear something a bit more comfortable tomorrow."

"What time will you be picking me up in the morning?" she wanted to know.

"Is six too early?"

She stifled a groan at what sounded like an ungodly hour, but said, "No. I'll be ready."

Stepping out of the car, she turned back and leaned down to meet his gaze. "Thank you for today. I really do appreciate it, and I know Mom would, too."

He gave a rough nod, remaining silent.

"Good night."

"'Night," he said softly.

She closed the car door and made her way up the steps to the front of the house. She hadn't left the porch light on when they left that morning, so she moved slowly up the steps and used the tiny pen light attached to her key ring to unlock the door.

Creed remained at the curb, his Mercedes idling softly, until she'd gotten inside, locked the door behind her and waved from the kitchen window to let him know she was all right. She couldn't tell for sure, but she thought he raised a hand to wave back before pulling away.

The old Creed, the one she'd known half her life, wouldn't have been as considerate. Oh, he'd have made sure she got home safely, but once he'd dropped her off, she'd have likely been on her own.

This Creed, the new one, as she was coming to think of him ever since they'd begun this strange, tentative new relationship, seemed more considerate, more compassionate.

With her, at least. With his family, he'd always been happy and outgoing, but with her he'd always acted more gruff and closed off.

She didn't know what had changed, exactly, except for her mother's sudden disappearance. But even then, her mother had been missing for months now, whereas he had only started coming around and being more courteous with her recently.

It was probably just the sex, she thought, making her way through the house. She left her purse and jacket in the kitchen, knowing she would need them again first thing in the morning, then headed upstairs. With each step, she loosened another item of clothing, making it easier for her to strip and fall straight into bed.

The minute she hit the mattress, she sighed with relief. She would have no trouble falling asleep tonight, as tired as she was.

Since Creed was her first lover, she couldn't claim to be an expert in the field of sex and how it affected people's personalities. But it was the only thing she could put her finger on that might explain why Creed's attitude toward her had changed. Not suddenly, but enough to be noticeable.

And truth be told, she didn't care. Even if he was only being nice to her and doing all of this to help find her mother because he either felt guilty for sleeping with her at all, or because he acted this way with all the women he slept with, she was simply grateful. And if it didn't last…well, she would deal with that when the time came, she supposed.

For now, though, she found great strength in his presence and support. Her life had been so strained and stressful lately, it felt good to be able to lean on him a bit. It felt good to not be quite so alone.

She had never *really* been alone, she knew that. The rest of the Fortunes, especially Nash, were as upset and concerned about Patricia as she was. But since she'd always felt like an outsider thrown into the middle of the close-knit Fortune clan, and because she and her mother were so close, she'd felt especially isolated since Patricia had gone missing.

Creed made her feel as though someone understood what she was going through, and that there might be a light at the end of the tunnel.

It was difficult not to let her heart and imagination read more into his behavior than there was. Already she could feel herself slipping, feel herself *wanting* to believe she was in love with him—really in love with him, not merely suffering the residual effects of her childhood crush—and that he might come to love her, too.

But each time her mind started to flit off into those flights of fancy, she tried her best to rein it in and once again plant both feet firmly in reality.

No matter what happened, she decided, as she began to drift off, she could never be sorry for giving him her virginity…and her heart.

Even if he wasn't willing to give her his in return.

* * *

Bright and early the next day they set out again in search of her mother. This time they had a list of some of Patricia's acquaintances, both past and present, and also decided to stop at every hotel and motel they came across in their travels, on the off chance a woman fitting Patricia's description had checked in or out or been seen in the area.

By noon, Maya was once again wiped out and didn't know how she could possibly go another six or eight hours. She was also beginning to feel as though the search for her mother was a lost cause and they would all have to just sit back and wait for Patricia to return on her own.

The only thing that kept her going was the fear that her mother might really be in trouble and *need* help. Until Maya knew for sure what was going on, she couldn't stop looking.

"How about some lunch?" Creed cut into her thoughts to ask.

He was dressed more casually today, in a pair of tan chinos and a light blue cotton button-down shirt. From her side of the car, though, he looked just as weary and frustrated as she felt.

"Sounds good," she said, thinking that a bite to eat and a gallon or two of caffeine were exactly what they needed to get through the rest of the day.

They found a nice sit-down restaurant that seemed to cater to families, and parked near the front entrance.

Creed laid a hand at the small of her back, sending shivers of awareness up and down her spine as they walked inside. He kept it there until the hostess had seen them to their seats, only letting his arm drop when they slid into opposite sides of the low booth. A waitress brought menus and took their drink orders, leaving them alone again.

"I was hoping we'd have found something by now," he said as they studied the list of lunch specials.

"Me, too. I just can't believe that no one has seen or heard from Mom at all. She's not the type of person I would have expected to be able to disappear without a trace."

Creed's mouth turned down in a frown. "Yeah. It's not like she's a ninja or ghost for the CIA or something."

Even though the situation was far from amusing, that made her chuckle. "No, she's definitely neither of those things, but she sure is doing a good job of staying hidden."

The waitress reappeared then to deliver two tall glasses of iced tea and finish jotting down their orders.

"Are you sure there isn't anything you can remember that might give us a better idea of where to look?" he asked as soon as the woman left.

Her brows knit, every muscle in her body tensing. Taking a breath, she forced herself to relax, knowing he didn't mean the question to sound like an accusation. They were both frustrated and worried and grabbing at any straw they could find that might lead them to Patricia.

"No, I'm sorry," she said with a shake of her head. Reaching for her tea, she took a sip before continuing. "She never said anything to me about leaving. Nothing that would have made me think going away was in her plans or that might hint at her whereabouts. Honestly, Creed, I'm as confused about all this as you are."

Their sandwiches arrived, and they ate in silence for a while. Then Maya set down her sandwich and said, "You have to understand that all of this has come as a huge shock for me. Mom's running off was bad enough, but then you drop the bomb on me that my father is still alive. I had no idea, and if my mother could keep that information a secret all these years, then she certainly could have refrained from letting anything slip about her plans to leave town."

Creed nodded, chewing thoughtfully. "It definitely came as a shock."

"Poor Nash. He's beside himself with worry. I feel so bad for him. And he really does love my mother."

"Yes. He does."

"My father—Wilton—didn't, I don't think. Maybe at one time, but from everything I remember of him, he was drunk and violent most of the time. Any little thing could set him off, and he always took his anger out on Mom."

"Did he ever hit you?" Creed asked.

She shook her head and swallowed what had turned out to be a delicious sandwich. "Not that I remember. I remember the yelling and hitting, Mom crying. There were a lot of times when she'd send me to my room so I wouldn't see what was going on, or take me away from the house for a while until the worst of one of Wilton's rages had blown over. Then one day, she sat me down, explained that my father had died, and told me we were going away."

"Where did your mother take you when she wanted to get you away from your father's temper?" he asked before biting into a crunchy chip.

"Different places," she said with a shrug. "It was always off the reservation, because if we'd stayed there and he came looking for us, he would have found us in no time. So she would take me to the library in town, or sometimes to the park. We didn't have much money, so anywhere we went had to be extremely cheap or free."

"The town outside the reservation," he murmured. "Would that happen to be one of the small towns we drove through yesterday on the way there and back?"

"Yes, I think so," she told him slowly. "Why?"

"We didn't check there. There was no reason to. But if Patricia is running scared, hiding from Wilton, maybe she went to one of the places where she used to feel safe."

A lump formed in Maya's throat, and she didn't think she could take another bite if she tried. Laying her sandwich carefully on the plate, she used the napkin from her lap to wipe her hands.

"Do you really think so?"

"I don't know," he replied, mimicking her actions

and then reaching into his pocket for his wallet. "But it's worth checking out."

He threw a large bill on the table, more than enough to cover the cost of their meals and a generous tip, before sliding out of the bench seat. "Were you finished?"

Even if she hadn't been, she suspected he probably would have dragged her out anyway. But she nodded eagerly and hurried to her feet, any sense of hunger or weariness gone in her anxiousness to get back on the road and check the two new places her mother might have gone.

It took them nearly an hour to reach Delmont. The Yankton Indian Reservation was only a few miles farther southwest, but they weren't going that far.

Driving slowly down the main street of town, Maya studied all the shop fronts and side streets, racking her brain for memories from the past. Some things looked more familiar than others, but she couldn't be sure if it was from her childhood or because they'd driven through only the day before.

"Do you remember how to get to the library?" Creed asked, keeping a hawk's eye on the sidewalks and people bustling by.

"No. It's been too long. Maybe we could stop and ask someone."

Instead they drove around a while longer until they spotted a blue-and-white sign with an arrow and the image of a person reading a book. Two signs later they were at the library.

It was a small brick building with brightly colored flowers lining a short concrete walk. The parking lot was large enough for only about three cars, and the tires of Creed's Mercedes ground loudly on the gravel as they pulled up.

"Looks like it's open," he said as they got out of the car and spotted the hours of operation posted inside one of the windows.

He pulled open the swinging glass door, then held it while she stepped inside. Although it had been many years and the setup of the library had changed, memories of being here with her mother flooded Maya.

Like libraries everywhere, the room was hushed and quiet. There was a woman sitting behind a long counter, carding books, and a couple of kids on the floor in one corner, flipping through picture books while their mother perused cookbooks at a nearby table.

"You look over there," he whispered, pointing to the right. "I'll check things out over here."

Moving in opposite directions, they walked up and down the rows of neatly lined stacks and peeked into several auxiliary rooms. They met back where they'd started, each shaking their head to show they hadn't found Patricia.

"Let me ask the librarian if she's seen your mother."

Striding to the circulation desk, Creed smiled as the woman stopped what she was doing and stood.

"Can I help you?" she asked.

"Yes. I'm looking for someone and wondered if

you'd seen her." He pulled a photo from the back pocket of his pants and showed it to her.

The woman studied it for a second, her brows knitting together in contemplation. "I don't…well, maybe. Yes, yes, I think she might have been in here. The hair isn't quite right," she continued, handing the picture back, "but if this is the woman I'm thinking of, she comes in quite a bit. She never checks out any books, but she'll sit right over there and read for hours, and sometimes she takes one of our on-your-honor paperbacks. She always brings them back, too, before taking the next."

At the woman's words, Maya's heart picked up its pace. She moved forward until she was standing directly beside Creed, whose own tall frame fairly vibrated with excitement. On top of the counter, his long fingers curled into fists while she twisted her hands together at her waist.

"When was the last time she came in?" Creed wanted to know.

"This morning. She only stayed for a bit, and took another book with her."

"Do you have any idea where she might have gone?"

"No, I'm sorry," the woman said, shaking her head sadly.

"All right," he said with a sigh. "You've been very helpful, thank you."

Putting a hand on Maya's back, he steered her toward the door and outside.

"What do we do now?" she asked, going to the passenger side of the car and sliding in as Creed did the same.

"I say we drive around, looking for her, maybe stop and ask a few more people if they've seen her. If nothing turns up, we can always come back here and stake out the place. Patricia's bound to come back to return that book she borrowed."

Her stomach was doing flips and she couldn't seem to stop fidgeting. "Do you really think the woman the librarian has been seeing is Mom?"

"I don't know," he replied, starting the engine and pulling slowly out of the parking lot, "but we're going to stick around until we find out for sure."

For the next thirty minutes they drove around town, up and down every street, looking for anyone who looked even remotely like Patricia. They stopped several times to double-check women they saw on the sidewalk, and even more often to run into small businesses to flash Patricia's picture and ask if anyone had seen her recently.

Frustration started to seep through her again, but she fought it off, reminding herself of Creed's plan to stake out the library, if necessary.

She was scanning the area, turning her head from one side to the other, when something caught her attention.

"Stop!"

Creed slammed on the breaks, and only after the car came to a screeching halt did Maya bother to glance in the side mirror and heave a sigh of relief that no one was driving behind them.

"What?" he wanted to know. "What did you see?"

"I'm not sure, but…" She raised a hand and pointed out the windshield. "I think that might be the park she used to take me to."

It was straight ahead, tucked along a side street and taking up about two full blocks. As they pulled closer and eased into a parallel parking space along the curb, she saw a swing set, jungle gym, sand box and even a small basketball court.

A dozen children ran around, playing, yelling, having a grand old time. Teenagers in ratty clothes and backward baseball caps dribbled balls, rode skateboards and sat in small clutches sneaking cigarettes. The number of adults was at a minimum, and she suspected those belonged more to the younger kids than the older ones.

As soon as Creed cut the engine, she unbuckled her seat belt and jumped out. He met her at the front of the car.

"Do you see her?" he asked.

She scanned the park's inhabitants again. "No. But the park is pretty large, and she probably wouldn't want to be close to all this noise and activity, anyway. Let's walk around."

She was getting used to him touching her, both casually and with firm intent, so she didn't think anything of it when he placed a hand at the small of her back and let her move ahead of him. But when that hand slid to her elbow, then down her arm to clasp her hand, she nearly jumped. Holding hands *wasn't* something she was used to, not with Creed.

Now wasn't the time to analyze the gesture, though. She could do that later, after they'd—God willing—found her mother.

Still holding his hand, she started forward, entering the park and immediately beginning to scan faces. They passed the main play area and walked toward a more secluded spot with small trees, decorative flower beds, and benches where people could sit to read or enjoy the nice summer weather.

Several yards ahead, there was a woman sitting on one of the benches, her back to them. She was slender, with short dark hair, and wearing a pale-pink light-weight sweater over a white blouse. Both looked well worn and oft washed. As they passed, Maya noticed the woman was reading a thick paperback novel.

They were getting closer, she thought with a tiny sigh. They'd found the park her mother had brought her to as a child, and they'd found a woman reading a book. If they were lucky, maybe the next reader they came across in this park would be Patricia.

Unfortunately, as they finished searching the park fifteen minutes later, she had to give up any hope of getting lucky. Her mother was nowhere to be found.

Following the same path they'd taken through the park, they once again passed the woman reading. She didn't pay any attention to them, but as she lifted a hand to turn to the next page of her book, the thin gold bracelet on her right wrist glinted in the afternoon sun, and Maya stopped in her tracks.

"Oh, my God. *Mom.*"

Nine

If it hadn't been for the bracelet, which Maya identified as one of Patricia's favorites, she never would have recognized the woman sitting on the bench as her mother.

Her hair was both darker and much shorter than it had been before she'd run away. Patricia had always kept regular salon appointments, her stylish bob almost a trademark.

But since she'd been gone, she'd apparently cut her hair herself. It was spiky and a bit uneven, and looked as though she'd colored it—two shades darker than her natural tone—with one of those box kits sold at every drugstore.

Maya squeezed Creed's fingers once, hard, before

releasing him and racing forward. At her breathless exclamation, the woman on the park bench raised her head and gasped, eyes going wide, book sliding from her limp hands to fall to the ground.

"Mom! Oh, my God, Mom, we've been so worried." She threw her arms around Patricia, hugging her tight.

They sat that way for a very long time, laughing, crying, rocking together. When they finally pulled apart, Maya wiped the tears from her face with her sleeve, refusing to let go of her mother's hands for even a second, afraid she would slip away again.

Patricia's own face was damp and blotchy, twin trails of wetness continuing to roll down her cheeks.

"What are you doing here?" her mother asked, her voice rough with emotion. "How did you find me?"

Maya turned her gaze to Creed, who stood only a few inches away. She could see the relief in his eyes, along with a light furrow to his brow and the line of concern thinning his lips.

Turning back to her mother, she said, "We've been looking for you for weeks now. We've all been so worried, and Nash is beside himself."

Patricia's own lips quivered, her lashes glittering with fresh tears. "You shouldn't have come. I can't go back, and I don't want you to get involved."

"It's all right," Maya assured her, patting the back of her mother's hand. "We know everything. Or almost everything. We know about Wilton—that he's still alive and has been blackmailing you. That is why you ran away, isn't it?"

At Maya's revelation, Patricia shuddered, the moisture gathered in her eyes spilling over. She threw herself once again into her daughter's arms and cried as if her life was ending.

When she finally calmed enough to straighten, her breathing was ragged, her chest hitching as she tried to compose herself.

"I'm sorry. Sorry I lied to you and ran away, and... I'm so sorry for everything."

"It's all right. We understand." She cast a quick glance over her shoulder at Creed to make sure he was still there, still offering his complete support. "No one is mad at you, I promise. We were all just worried about you, and afraid for you, and missed you very much."

Creed stepped forward, taking a seat on the bench on the other side of Patricia. "It really will be all right, Patricia. We're here to take you home."

"No, I can't," Patricia said resolutely. "Nash will hate me when he finds out that I lied about being widowed. And Wilton is still out there. He could ruin me, ruin us. You don't understand—"

"Nash doesn't hate you, Mom," Maya told her. "He loves you very much and wants you to come home."

"And Wilton Blackstone won't be bothering you anymore," Creed put in firmly. "We know about the blackmail. We have proof of it, and he's been arrested.

We'll see that he's punished and make sure he never comes near you again."

He reached out to touch her, his large hand dwarfing Patricia's slender, sloping shoulder. "I give you my word, and the word of the entire Fortune family. We'll see that you're protected."

Patricia looked at Creed and then Maya, studying their expressions for the truth in their words. Her tears had dried, her breathing regulated and interrupted only by the occasional sniff.

"But Nash—"

"Nash loves you," Maya said. "He could never hate you. He might be upset that you misled him, and about your marriage not being valid, but he won't hate you. And I think that if you explain things to him, he'll understand."

"Do you really think so?" Patricia asked in a watery voice.

Before Maya could answer, Creed said, "Absolutely. We all love you, Patricia. Let us take you home so we can show you how much."

When they reached Sioux Falls, Patricia asked if they could stop at Maya's house first so she could clean up before returning to the Fortune Estate.

They'd stopped at the small house in Delmont where Patricia had most recently been renting a room, to collect her meager belongings. Since her clothes were now looking quite faded and threadbare from having been worn and washed so many times during the months she'd been missing, Maya helped her find some things from her own closet.

Patricia was quiet the rest of the way home, staring out the window and holding her hands together tightly in her lap.

Maya understood her anxiety. Her mother was about to see her husband for the first time in months, having to bare her soul and admit that their marriage of thirteen years had never been legal. Her own stomach was churning; she could only imagine how terrifying the prospect must be for Patricia.

Of course, her own discomfort wasn't due entirely to what her mother was going through right now. She was equally distracted by thoughts of the effect Patricia's return might have on her relationship with Creed.

As much as she'd missed her mother and worried about her while she was missing, Maya had to admit she'd enjoyed the change in Creed's attitude toward her and the time he'd been spending with her recently. But now that Patricia was back and the crisis of her disappearance was passing, there would be no reason for him to drop by her house anymore or call just to check on her.

Swallowing hard, she blinked until the stinging behind her eyes dissipated. She would miss him, miss having him in her life in a capacity other than surly stepbrother.

To say nothing of how much she would miss sharing her bed with him.

Creed made a right turn off the main road onto the long, circular crushed stone drive that led to the Fortune Estate. Her insides began to tighten as soon as the sprawling mansion came into view, almost as though her body sensed the sand in the hourglass of her happiness running out.

When Creed pulled up in front of the house and cut the engine, they all got out and slowly walked inside without bothering to knock. Silence surrounded them, and for a moment they simply stood in the middle of the foyer, no one making a move to go farther or look to see who might be home.

At her side, Patricia squeezed Maya's hand so hard, the fingers were starting to tingle.

"It's all right," Maya whispered, returning the pressure and patting Patricia's arm. "Nash will understand, and Creed and I will stay with you the entire time, if you want us to."

Creed added a supporting hand to Patricia's back as they started forward.

They hadn't taken more than three or four steps when a noise at the top of the wide double stairwell caused them all to look up.

Nash stood frozen on the landing, staring down at them, a look of utter shock on his face. A second later he raced the rest of the way down the stairs.

"Patricia! Oh, dear God, Patricia. I thought I would never see you again."

Patricia released Maya's hand and flew across the

foyer, meeting Nash halfway. They kissed and hugged, both crying with delight at being together again after such a long and stressful separation.

Maya felt tears well in her own eyes, and sniffed to hold them at bay. Beside her, Creed was grinning, rocking back on his heels with his arms linked across his chest.

He knew as well as she did that there were still a few bumps in the road ahead for her mother and his father, but right now, at this very moment in time, there was only happiness, relief and cause for celebration.

When Nash and Patricia finally parted, they were bleary-eyed and sniffing, but smiling from ear to ear.

"Where have you been?" Nash wanted to know, holding her by the shoulders.

The question made Patricia tense, and Maya took a single step forward, ready to support her mother. But before Maya could come to her rescue, Patricia steeled her spine and looked Nash straight in the eye.

"That's something I need to explain," she told him, "and I can only hope you don't hate me afterward."

Concern wrinkled Nash's brow, but his response was nothing less than Maya would have expected.

"I could never hate you, darling," he replied adamantly.

"Yes, well…" Patricia dried the undersides of her eyes with one thumb, then tucked a long strand of hair behind her ear. "You might want to wait until you've heard what I have to tell you before deciding that for sure."

Nash didn't look convinced, but Maya suspected

his spirits were too high at having his wife safely home to argue.

"Let's go into the library," Patricia said, taking him by the hand and leading him in that direction.

Maya's feet itched to follow. Her mother had been so worried, so frightened to come clean with Nash about everything, that Maya didn't want to leave her to face those fears alone.

Now that she was home, however, Patricia seemed more herself. It had taken only one glimpse of Nash for her mother to remember the love, the dedication, the man he was and the years they'd spent together.

Whatever his reaction to what Patricia was about to tell him, Maya had no doubt that his adoration for her mother would overshadow it all. If not immediately, then eventually.

When they reached the library, Patricia turned back in her direction and offered a small smile. "Thank you for everything, but I'll be fine now. You two go on."

Before Maya could respond, her mother closed the heavy pocket doors, leaving her alone in the wide foyer with Creed.

"Well," he said with a shrug, "I guess our job is done."

She nodded absently, her gaze still locked on the library door as though she could see through the thick wooden panel. Even though Patricia had told them it was okay to go, it didn't feel right to Maya to simply take off. Not yet. Not until she knew for sure that everything between Nash and her mother would be all right.

Taking the decision out of her hands, Creed took her by the shoulders and physically turned her in the opposite direction.

"Let's get something to drink, then call the rest of the family. They'll all want to know Patricia is back and okay."

They made their way to the kitchen, where several members of the household staff were busy preparing dinner. Creed asked for drinks to be brought to the great room, then steered Maya in that direction.

"Do you think Nash will forgive her?" she asked, standing awkwardly in the doorway, keeping her hands in her pockets to avoid the urge to fidget.

"Yes, I do."

At the conviction in his tone, she lifted her head and met his eyes. They hit her like a ton of bricks, as always. And as always, she felt her limbs go weak, liquid heat pooling low in her belly.

"If there's one thing you can be sure of," he went on, "it's that my dad loves your mother. He may not be happy that she lied to him from the beginning, and continued to mislead him throughout their marriage, but he'll understand. They'll work it out."

Their drinks arrived then, and Maya had to move farther into the room to get out of the servant's way as the young woman carried a tray of iced tea to a nearby table.

"You use that phone," Creed said, pointing to the

sleek princess land line across the room. "I'll use my cell. We'll reach everyone faster if we divvy up the calls. Which ones do you want?"

After agreeing which Fortune family members they would each call, Maya took one of the glasses of tea and began dialing, spending the next half hour informing Creed's siblings that Patricia was home. The news was met each time with joy and relief, and every single one of the family members wanted to know where they'd found her, where she'd been and why she'd left in the first place.

Maya could hear bits and pieces of Creed's conversations, and knew he was promising them the same thing she was—that they would fill in the blanks as soon as they were all together. It certainly beat telling the same story over and over again, and until Nash and Patricia came out of the library, they weren't confident of exactly how things would end.

Twenty minutes after they finished making the phone calls, they heard car doors and then the front door slam open as Fortunes started pouring into the house. Leaving their empty glasses to be refilled when drinks were brought for everyone, Maya and Creed made their way back to the foyer to greet the others.

Creed placed a hand at the small of her back as they walked, and Maya couldn't decide if she found the gesture comforting or disturbing. Maybe a little of both. Comforting because she was growing used to his presence, used to the place he'd made for himself in her life.

And disturbing because she wanted so much for him to remain in that place, even though she knew it wasn't possible.

As they neared the entryway, she felt Creed's touch fall away. She missed it immediately but was sharp enough to realize that he'd pulled back because he didn't want any of the rest of the family to notice anything out of the ordinary.

It hurt, which Maya found ironic, considering that she didn't want anyone else to know they'd been involved, either. It would just complicate matters that were already plenty complicated enough.

She wanted Creed, but couldn't have him. And he didn't want her at all, not really.

Unrequited love, she was unfortunately learning, was both painful and illogical.

Sadness lying like a stone at the bottom of her stomach, she pasted a smile on her face and hugged both Gina and Case, who were the first to arrive.

Gina's face was flushed with excitement, and Maya thought she saw a tell-tale rim of red around the woman's eyes, as though she'd recently been crying. Gina wasn't a Fortune by blood—of course, neither was Maya, so they had that in common—but she'd been just as worried about Patricia's disappearance as everyone else.

She also had pregnancy hormones running rampant through her system, probably adding to the ease with which she burst into tears. According to Case, something as simple as running out of milk could cause a near breakdown these days.

Eliza and Reese, Blake and Sasha, Skylar and Zack, and Diana and Max all showed up in short order, within minutes of each other. Each time a new couple burst through the front door, it was a repeat of the first— embraces all around, damp eyes and a thousand questions about where Patricia was and what was going on.

Once things had calmed down a bit and everyone who was expected to make an appearance arrived, Creed took command, drawing everyone into the great room, calling for refreshments, then explaining the entire situation in a low, even voice. He started by telling them about the information the investigators had uncovered, followed by their own personal search for Patricia and how they'd finally found her.

He left out any mention of the time he'd spent at her house recently…or in her bed…sticking strictly to the facts of the search and Patricia's return.

The news of Maya's father still being alive and Patricia's marriage to Nash being illegal and invalid stunned them all, Maya could tell.

But just as Creed had been understanding and supportive of the situation, so were the rest, which added to her sense of relief. She didn't want anyone thinking less of her mother for something that had not only gotten its start a decade before, but that Patricia had felt was her only option at the time.

Creed finished by informing the group at large that

Nash and Patricia were locked in the library, having a long-overdue discussion and hopefully working things out between them.

"I don't know about you," Case said, raising his glass of pale brown tea, "but I could sure go for something stronger than this."

Creed, who was standing beside him gave his own glass a gentle shake, sending ice cubes clinking. With a harsh laugh, he said, "No kidding. Tell you what, when Dad comes out of that library, we'll crack open a bottle of scotch. I'm guessing he'll need a drink by then, too."

"Deal."

Without planning or conscious thought, the women gathered in one corner while the men drifted to another. Conversation was stilted and uncomfortable; they were all trying to act normal and upbeat, but a cloud of uncertainty hung over the room.

Even so, Maya was struck once again by how these people—whom she'd never felt close to before—seemed to come together as a single unit for a mutual cause. They were, in a word, family.

A lump formed in her throat as she thought of how she used to consider them cold and distant. She certainly couldn't pin those labels on them now. They were anything but aloof as they struggled to maintain a sense of regularity and put each other at ease.

And she had to wonder: Had they changed—or had she?

From the time she and her mother had moved into this giant house with the Fortunes, she'd felt like an outsider, but they definitely weren't making her feel like one now. She was one of them, included and cared for.

She took a sip of tea, as much to wash away the emotion threatening to overwhelm her as to buy a little time to put her rapid-fire thoughts in order.

Looking back now, she realized this wasn't the first time she'd been included by the Fortune siblings, made to feel as though she truly belonged. She'd simply been so used to feeling left out that she assumed she was, even when these people were trying their best to help her fit in.

No, that wasn't it, either. They weren't trying to do anything…they just *were.* They were treating her like family because to them she *was* family.

A wave of love and appreciation washed over her so keenly she nearly fumbled the glass in her hands.

They were family, and she was a part of it. They were *her* family, and she loved each and every one of them with a strength and devotion she hadn't even realized she possessed until this moment.

It was a revelation, and she thanked God for it.

If only her relationship with Creed could be as quickly and easily resolved, but she had a feeling that would take twenty years to puzzle itself out, too.

She was about to sigh with resignation when the entire room went quiet as a tomb. Noticing the direction of the others' gazes, she turned to find Nash and Patricia standing in the doorway.

Her mother's face was streaked with tears, and Nash's eyes were bleary, as though he, too, had been crying. Their hands were joined, she noticed, which had to be a good sign.

All the same, Maya held her breath, waiting to hear what they would say.

Nash cleared his throat. I'm glad you're all here," he said. "Patricia and I have some things we need to tell you."

The good news was that Nash and Patricia were going to be all right. Nash had been more upset with Patricia for running away instead of trusting him enough to tell him the truth than he was that she'd lied to him to begin with. She was now strictly forbidden from ever keeping anything from him again, to which she'd chuckled and tearily agreed.

Once the family had been assured that everything was okay and life would likely be returning to normal, they'd celebrated in true Fortune style. Bottles of wine and scotch had been uncorked and passed around, and platters of cookies and cakes and other finger foods had been served.

Creed took another long swallow of the hundred-year-old Scotch that was his father's favorite, letting it burn a trail down his throat.

He should be relieved. Hell, he should be celebrating right along with everyone else…. God knew he had more to be grateful for. Not only for Patricia's safe return and an end to the mystery of where she'd run off to for so long, but his freedom from whatever spell Maya had woven around him the past few weeks.

There wasn't a hope in hell of breaking free of the spell she'd cast over him for the past twenty years, but after sating his initial passions with Maya, he'd only continued seeing her, continued *sleeping* with her, because she'd needed someone.

That's what he'd told himself, anyway.

He'd also told himself that as soon as Patricia was safe and sound back home, he'd put an end to his secret, clandestine affair with her daughter.

Well, they'd found Patricia and brought her home, so that's exactly what he intended to do.

All might not be perfect or completely settled, but it was good enough that Maya didn't need him anymore. With her mother back, and the truth of Wilton's blackmail out in the open, she was no longer vulnerable, no longer worried, no longer in need of a strong shoulder to lean on.

Or anything else he might have to offer.

This was good. Better than good; it was great. It had been the plan all along.

Now all he had to do was stick to it.

And he would, although his body seemed to have other ideas.

While everyone else was crowded around Patricia, welcoming her home and promising to stand by her through thick and thin, he'd made the mistake of glancing in Maya's direction. She'd been watching the scene, her eyes sparkling with emotion, the hint of a smile on her lips.

It was the first time he'd ever seen her look quite like that around his family. Serene, at ease…happy.

He wanted to think it was her expression that had stirred him, but he knew it was much more than that. *She* stirred him. Her strength, her poise, her quiet beauty. All the same qualities that had stirred him from the time she'd hit puberty, maybe earlier.

But now he knew so much more about her. He knew what she looked like naked and the noises she made in the throes of passion. He knew what made her toes curl, her nipples pucker and her eyes flutter closed on a sigh of ecstasy.

He knew, and he damn well couldn't forget. Would never forget.

Which was only going to make walking away that much harder.

He tossed back the last of the scotch, hoping it would dull the ache throbbing at his temples and his gut.

Walking away wouldn't be easy, but then, he'd known that from the start.

Just like living under the same roof with her all these years hadn't been easy. He'd watched her grow up; watched her blossom; watched her fail and succeed, make mistakes and soldier through them. It hadn't been easy to be forced to see her on a regular basis, even after they'd both moved away from the Fortune Estate, and to be slapped in the face with the fact that she was family—his stepsister, for God's sake—when he wished she could be so much more.

It was enough to make a man want to crawl into a bottle and never come out. And since his glass was currently empty…

He pushed himself up from the wing chair where he'd been sitting, listening with only half an ear to the conversations going on around him, and headed to the bar for a refill. Just as he was recapping the bottle of hundred-year-old scotch, Blake sauntered up.

Creed tipped the bottle in his half brother's direction and lifted a brow, silently asking if Blake wanted some before he put it away.

"No, thanks, I'll stick with what I've got," Blake said, gesturing with his still-full glass.

Creed replaced the scotch in its spot amongst the other assorted bottles on the bar, then took a sip while he waited for Blake to say whatever was on his mind. And from the look on his face, it was obvious there was something.

"I thought you should know that my mom has managed to lasso herself another rich husband," Blake told him, speaking of his mother and Nash's second wife, Trina Watters Fortune. "They're jetting off to Europe as soon as the ink is dry on the marriage license."

"I guess that's good news," Creed said. "At least she seems to have given up on trying to get Dad back and will be out of everyone's hair over there."

Blake nodded grimly, taking a drink before continuing. "Look, I want to apologize for the mess she made of everyone's lives. I didn't want to believe she was capable of some of the things she was doing, but, well…I was wrong, and I'm sorry I didn't see that sooner."

"Apology accepted," Creed replied easily. "But only if you'll accept mine for making you pay for Trina's manipulations. You weren't responsible for your mother's actions, even though I treated you as though you were." Regret narrowed his eyes and thinned his lips. "You can't know how sorry I am for that, and I hope you can forgive me. I'd like for us to start over and be real brothers from now on." Glancing over at Nash, his other brother, and his brothers-in-law, along with the women who had just begun to trickle back into the room, Creed offered a small smile. "A man can never have too much family."

For a second Blake didn't reply. Then he cleared his throat and held out his hand. "I'd like that," he said, his voice rough with feeling. "A lot."

Creed shifted his drink to the opposite hand so they could shake on it. Before letting go, though, he couldn't resist giving his younger brother a last, serious warning.

"One more thing," he said, his tone somber as he tightened his grip. "You'd better take good care of Sasha."

Even though they'd spent a good amount of time dating, Creed had never really had a romantic interest in Sasha Kilgore. They'd gone out and pretended to be seriously involved only to keep other, cloying women away from him.

She'd done him a favor in that, and they were friends. Good friends. He didn't want to see anything happen to her.

Not that he thought Blake would ever do anything to intentionally hurt his new fiancée. Blake was entirely too smitten with the gorgeous redhead.

Creed couldn't blame him, but a word of caution was still in order.

"She's a hell of a woman," he continued. "She deserves only the best, and if you make her cry, I'll have to pound you. That's what big brothers do."

"Don't worry," Blake said, casting a glance at Sasha as she entered into the room carrying a tray of hastily made hors d'oeuvres.

She was grinning broadly at something Skylar had said, waddling along pregnantly at her side, and Blake's eyes filled with a glint that could only be described as complete and total adoration. "I intend to take very good care of her."

Creed lifted his drink to his mouth to cover a smile. "Glad to hear it."

"For the record," Blake said, dragging his gaze from the woman he loved, "I think Maya is a pretty terrific woman, too. She'd be good for you, if only you'd see it and take the initiative to do something about it."

Creed froze, the scotch in his mouth trickling a burning path down his throat as he struggled to swallow and then breathe. When he finally managed, it was with a cough, and his voice was strained when he tried to speak.

"What are you talking about?" he demanded.

"I know," Blake said, shaking his head, "we're all supposed to pretend we don't know that you're attracted to her. Unfortunately, no one in this family is blind. We've all seen the way you look at her, and though we've never talked about it, I think everyone would agree that it's time you stop moping around, watching her from afar, and just went for it."

A low throb was beginning to pound behind Creed's eye sockets. "Don't be ridiculous," he snapped. "She's our sister."

"Stepsister," Blake corrected. "Related only by Dad's marriage to Patricia, which is no true relation at all. And, hell, it turns out they're not even married now. You need to stop worrying so much about that sort of thing and focus on what's important. If you care about her—and I think you do—then you need to do something about it. Toss her over your shoulder and drag her to bed, then marry her before some other lucky bastard beats you to the punch. She'd make you a great wife."

Blake chuckled and took a small sip of his drink. "Think of it this way," he added. "At least you don't have to suffer through the misery of meeting her parents and introducing her to your own. Or dealing with in-laws. That's all a done deal, and we know and love her already."

With that Blake drained his glass, set it down on the sideboard and walked away to join Sasha.

Creed stood there, watching as his brother slipped a hand around his fiancée's waist and leaned in to press a kiss to her temple. Sasha tipped her head to smile up at him, utter happiness shining in her green eyes and emanating from every pore of her body.

Blake's words echoed through his head, making the pounding even worse and keeping time with the frenetic beat of his heart.

He stood there for what seemed like forever, observing all the couples in the room. And suddenly he was envious. Everyone had someone. Everyone was happily married, or on their way to it.

Everyone, that was, except him.

He'd never thought of himself as being the marrying kind before, never thought in terms of a serious, lasting relationship or settling down with one woman. *The* woman, who seemed to suit him like no other, who fit into his life and his world as comfortably as an old pair of jeans.

But he wanted it, he realized.

It was like a flash of lightning in the night sky, hitting him hard and fast right in the solar plexus.

He wanted that, and he wanted it with Maya.

Ten

Creed was unusually quiet on the drive home, and since Maya was both physically exhausted and emotionally drained from the day's events, she was more than happy to remain silent herself. She let her head rest against the back of the seat and watched the scenery outside the side window, hoping the tension running through her body didn't show.

The trip back to her house also gave her time to decide exactly how to tell Creed it was over. Whatever had been going on between them these past few weeks, she needed to break it off, be done with it, stop letting him tie her up in knots.

She'd been wondering what would happen to this so-called relationship they'd been having, until she'd

looked over at him earlier this evening during the celebration of her mother's return. Glancing in his direction,
she'd caught him watching her. The look in his blue
eyes had sent her heart rate into triple digits, but it
hadn't lasted long.

He'd blinked, and the heat was gone, replaced by a
cool, impassive expression. Arching one dark brow,
he'd lifted his glass of scotch to his lips and turned
away.

It was the same way he used to look at her, the same
way he used to act toward and around her. So it seemed
that whatever had passed between them these past few
weeks wasn't going to grow, wasn't going to blossom
into something deep and meaningful.

That's when she'd realized she needed to call it
quits…while she still had her dignity and a chance to
put the pieces of her upside-down life back together.

She might not like it, and it wasn't how she would
have chosen to have things turn out, but she also wasn't
surprised. Whatever had compelled him to take her to
bed in the first place was obviously temporary, as she'd
known it would be.

It was probably even for the best. Now maybe she
could move on, get her life back to some semblance of
order and possibly develop a *normal* relationship with
another man, crossing Creed Fortune off her list of even
the most remote of possibilities.

And she was going to do it before he had the chance.
The end was near, she could feel it, but she would be

damned if she'd stand there and let *him* tell *her* all the reasons they couldn't be together anymore, all the reasons it would never work.

Ten minutes later Creed pulled the Mercedes up to the curb in front of her darkened town house and cut the engine. Without waiting for him to come around to her door, she got out and started up the steps, relieved when he followed her.

She stepped inside and flipped on a light, waiting for him to close the door behind him.

He didn't approach her, for which she was grateful. If he'd stalked toward her with that look in his eyes that said he couldn't wait to strip her bare and make love to her again, she wasn't sure she'd have been able to stand her ground and make him listen to what she'd decided she had to say.

But he simply stood there, just inside the closed front door, and watched her.

Setting her purse on the kitchen table, she wrapped her fingers around the back of one of the chairs for added support and said, "Thank you for all your help in finding my mother."

His expression didn't change, but he nodded almost imperceptibly. "You're welcome."

She swallowed, forcing herself to press on. "Creed, there's something I need to tell you."

His gaze flickered slightly, his eyes going a shade darker, but he said nothing, waiting for her to continue.

"I don't think we should see each other anymore."

She said the words in a rush, needing to get them out before her courage failed her.

She didn't know what type of reaction she'd been expecting from him, but it hadn't been complete silence. An argument maybe, or a creatively muttered curse. Instead, a muscle jumped in his jaw and he crossed his arms over his chest as he stared at her.

"We both know we've just been…passing time," she told him when the silence stretched out between them, jumbling her already strained nerves. "It was never going to last, and now that my mother is home, there's no need to continue spending time together. We'd only be…fooling ourselves and drawing unwanted attention."

Seconds ticked past while she waited for him to respond. She would take anything—a shout, a shrug, a string of expletives.

Eyes narrowed and mouth set, he dropped his arms, then said, "You're probably right."

Her stomach tightened at his calm acquiescence. She hadn't realized until that very moment that she wanted him to fight for her. Argue with her, yell at her, demand she not give up on them so easily.

Declare his undying love.

But, of course, that was never going to happen. She should simply be glad he wasn't going to make this any harder on her than it already was.

"I guess I'll see you, then," he said, turning to open the door.

She nodded, taking a step forward as though to see him out, even though there was no need.

"I promised my mom I'd attend Sunday dinner at the estate," she told him, then wanted to kick herself for letting him think she was counting the hours until she would see him again.

He stared at her a moment before inclining his head and walking away.

Closing the door behind him, she watched through the window as he walked down the sidewalk and around the hood of his car to slide in behind the wheel. Her lungs hitched, and she felt a tell-tale prickling of tears, but she didn't cry. If anything, she felt numb.

Breaking things off had been the right move. The only move, really, considering his lack of emotion about their relationship and the complete impossibility of a future for them.

But the young woman in her wept for the loss of a decade-long dream of true love, while the adult woman hardened her heart and steeled her spine to face a lifetime of loneliness.

Almost a week passed while Creed fluctuated between being relieved that Maya had ended things when she did…and being furious that she'd cast him aside so carelessly.

Hadn't he just begun to think that maybe he was ready to settle down and to do it with Maya? Not two hours before, hadn't he decided to sit her down and tell her flat-out that he thought they should continue seeing each other and find out where it would lead them?

Then she'd pulled the rug right out from under him by telling him she didn't want to see him anymore. That whatever they'd had was fun while it lasted, but she was ready to put it behind her.

At first he'd thought it was for the best. Had even been grateful he hadn't had to come up with the words to tell her much the same.

But the longer they were apart, the harder he tried to put the pieces of his life back to the way they'd been before he'd given in to temptation and taken Maya to bed, the less appreciative he became.

He missed her, dammit. Missed seeing her, talking with her…making love to her.

And as much as he'd fought it, he was no longer certain he wanted things to return to the way they'd been. He didn't want to see her at the estate, at Sunday dinners, and pretend she was nothing more than family, when he could close his eyes and picture her standing naked before him. Or feel the silk of her bronzed skin beneath his fingertips.

He ended up firing his receptionist twice while his brain tried to make sense of what he was feeling. Thankfully, she was used to his moods—which sometimes turned black and foul during business dealings, too—and chose to ignore him.

It was Case, though, who finally came to his office and told him to snap out of it. He suggested rather strongly that Creed either do something about whatever was making him such a bloody bear to deal with lately or get over it and stop being an ass.

Creed wasn't sure how to go about doing either, but he knew his brother was right.

Leaving work early, he went up to his apartment on the top floor of the Dakota Fortune office building and changed out of his standard business suit to a pair of tan chinos and a dark blue shirt.

Even though it was a bit early to start imbibing, he fixed himself a good, stiff drink of bourbon, then wandered restlessly around the penthouse. His blood felt too hot for his veins, simmering just below the surface, threatening to boil over.

The alcohol now sitting at the bottom of his stomach didn't help, either. Instead of calming him, it seemed to put him more on edge.

With a curse, he set his almost-full highball glass on a nearby credenza and grabbed his keys. Riding the elevator down to the underground parking garage, he climbed into his Mercedes and passed through the security gate onto the street.

He hadn't intended to drive to Maya's house, hadn't consciously thought to aim the car in that direction. But a few minutes later he found himself cruising down her block.

His fingers tightened on the steering wheel, twisting against the leather until his knuckles turned white. His stomach churned again, but this time it had nothing to do with the few sips of bourbon he'd consumed.

He eased to the curb, coming to a stop behind another car parked directly in front of Maya's town house. The black Lexus looked familiar, but he couldn't place it.

Cutting the engine, he sat there as the seconds ticked by, staring at her closed front door. He considered getting out of the car, walking up and ringing the doorbell, but he had no practical reason for being there. If anything, he should be avoiding her, except when that was impossible because of family functions.

But damned if he didn't want to see her again. Feel the satiny strands of her hair between his fingertips, smell the light, feminine scent that seemed to invade his pores whenever he was around her.

His hand was on the ignition—whether to turn the key or pull it out and take it with him, he wasn't sure— when Maya's front door opened and a man stepped out.

Brad McKenzie. And Maya was close on his heels, her hand resting lightly on his arm.

Creed saw red. Heat crawled up his neck and burned in his gut. His hands balled into fists.

What was that bastard doing here?

With Maya.

Touching her.

He was out of the car before he'd completed the thought, his vision still blurred with fury, his knuckles itching to make contact with the other man's jaw.

His strides ate up the yard or two of sidewalk between him and where Brad and Maya now stood.

"What the hell are you doing here?" he charged, startling both of them into spinning in his direction.

"Creed," Maya began.

But his attention was focused on Brad, whose own gaze narrowed and darkened when he saw Creed barreling toward him.

He recognized that expression—it was the look of a possessive man. A man who wanted to stake his claim, mark his territory.

And that territory was Maya.

Well, he couldn't have her. As far as Creed was concerned, she was already spoken for, and McKenzie could go take a flying leap. Over a very steep cliff, if he had his way.

Before another word could be uttered, Creed had McKenzie by the shirtfront, pushing him back a couple of steps as he raised his right arm, ready to throw the first punch.

"What are you doing?" Maya shouted, her eyes round with terror as she threw herself in front of Brad, shoving both hands at Creed's chest.

With Maya in the way, he couldn't pound the other man as he'd have liked. He lowered his arm but kept his hand balled in McKenzie's shirt.

"Stop it," Maya demanded, still pushing at his chest and now yanking at his arm to get him to let go of McKenzie. "Stop it, Creed, I mean it."

For long minutes time stood still. The muscles in Creed's arms bulged, and his teeth ground together. McKenzie didn't make a move against him, was just standing there. But he didn't look intimidated or afraid. If anything, he looked as if he'd enjoy it if Creed hit him, so he'd have an excuse to hit him back.

Taking a deep breath, Creed loosened his hold and dropped his arm to his side. Maya inserted herself more fully between them, and he retreated half a step to give her more room and keep her from being pressed up against Brad.

She was breathing heavily, her eyes flashing fire. But instead of laying into him, she stared at him for a moment, then turned to face McKenzie.

"I'm sorry, Brad, but I think you should go."

The man stood perfectly still for a beat, his gaze remaining locked on Creed. Then his eyes flicked to Maya and he nodded.

"I'll talk to you later," he said softly.

As soon as Brad was in his black Lexus and driving away, Maya hit Creed square in the chest.

"What is *wrong* with you?"

"What the hell was *he* doing here?" he growled in response.

"That's none of your business." Crossing her arms over her chest, she turned and headed back to the house.

"It damn well is my business," he told her, dogging her every step.

She didn't try to slam the door in his face, which surprised him. Instead she moved to the middle of the kitchen before twisting to face him, leaving him to slam the door himself after he'd stepped in behind her.

"Why? Why is it your business?"

"Because," he answered, his temper flaring before he'd fully formed his response. "It just is."

"No, Creed," she said, her voice turning low and calm. "It really isn't."

A shiver of dread ran through him, turning his blood icy as he watched her turn and walk out of the kitchen through the second entryway that led to the dining room and the rest of the house.

He'd spent the last decade pretending he didn't care about her and was pretty sure he'd spend the next decade kicking himself for all the time he'd wasted, all the time they'd lost because of his stubbornness and stupidity.

"Maya, wait."

He caught up to her at the base of the stairs and had to fight not to grab her up then and there.

It would have been a simple matter to wrap his fingers around her arm and drag her to him as his gut was urging him to do. But he didn't think he-man tactics were what the situation called for. He'd used quite enough of those over the past few weeks, and while they'd gotten him into Maya's bed, he didn't think they would win her over for a lifetime.

Sticking his hands deep into his front pockets to keep from reaching for her, he asked, "Do you want McKenzie? Is that it?"

With a sigh she said, "I don't know what I want. Brad's a nice guy. He really cared about me. But I've treated him terribly, and your little display of aggression out there certainly didn't help."

She rolled her eyes at him before continuing. "Which is why I was breaking up with him. He came over so we could talk, but I think we both knew we were never going to be more than friends. I don't think I'll ever be able to be more than friends with any man, thanks to you."

Her already-stiff posture turned even more rigid. "Happy now?"

It didn't take him a heartbeat to respond. "Yes."

Huffing out an angry, frustrated breath, she spun around and started to stomp up the steps.

"Don't you want to know why I'm happy?" he called after her.

"No, I really don't."

He followed her, climbing the stairs slowly, one at a time. Determination marked his every move.

She'd reached her bedroom, slamming the door behind her in an effort to shut him out, but he didn't let that stop him. Twisting the knob, he opened the door again and stepped inside.

Maya was on the other side of the room, standing with her back to him as she rummaged around in her closet, making an obvious effort to ignore him. Not that it was going to work.

"I'm in love with you," he said, the apprehension in his belly easing slightly when she froze in midmotion.

"I'm glad you broke things off with McKenzie. And I'm glad I've ruined you for other men if it means you'll be more likely to stay with me."

Seconds ticked past while he waited for her reaction, his lungs burning with the need for oxygen while he held his breath. Slowly she lowered her arm from where she'd been reaching for a top shelf of the closet and turned to face him.

"You don't really want me," she said, licking her lips to help get the words out. "You only slept with me to get me out of your system, remember?"

"I remember everything. Including the fact that I've wanted you since you started to change from a spindly kid to a full-grown woman."

"That's not true," she charged, her voice wavering. "You barely knew I existed."

"Oh, I knew. I treated you pretty badly back then— ignoring you a lot of the time, teasing you, censuring you. I was a jerk. I know that, and I'm sorry about it. My only excuse is that I wanted you. Even then, when you were too damn young to know the difference and I was definitely old enough to know better.

"I shouldn't have been attracted to you, though, and the guilt and frustration of the entire situation made me angry. More often than not, I took that anger out on you. I was a moody bastard, that's for sure," he said with a harsh laugh. "And I made your life miserable."

"Yes," she choked out, still looking shocked and numb, "you did."

"That was a long time ago, though. And now we've got this…" He waved a hand between them, indicating some invisible thread that seemed to tie them together, keep them bound, even when they each tried their best to break away. "Connection. This insatiable hunger for each other that isn't going away, no matter how much we might wish it would."

"You make me crazy," she said, shaking her head. Her lashes fluttered and her chest hitched slightly as she drew a breath. "You claim to be in love with me, then say you wish you weren't. You tell me you've wanted me for years, but until recently you acted like I was nothing more than a thorn in your side. Which is it, Creed? I'd really like to know so I can move on with my life."

He grinned at the sassy remark and took a step forward. Then another, until he was close enough to grasp her by the shoulders.

"That night a few weeks ago," he began. "You reminded me on the phone of the night when you were seventeen and I caught that boy trying to take advantage of you in the back seat of his car. I said some things after that—some nasty, hurtful things that you've been carrying around with you ever since. But I want you to know I didn't mean them."

His thumbs moved in small circles on the flesh of her upper arms, left bare by her short-sleeved top.

"None of it. I was furious that anyone would dare touch you like that, treat you like that. I wanted to kill that kid," he snarled, one corner of his mouth curling upward the way it had all those years ago.

"I was also sick with jealousy that you were dating at all. Because at the same time I didn't want any other boys near you, I couldn't come clean about wanting to be with you myself. But I'm older now, and I know what I want. I also know what I'm willing to risk to have it."

His grip on her arms tightened and he dragged her closer, until she was pressed to his chest, her face only inches from his own.

"I was so damn worried about what others would think and with protecting the Fortune family's reputation, that I almost let you get away. But I don't care about any of that anymore. I love you and want you to marry me."

He paused for a moment, sliding his hands from her shoulders to her temples, running his fingers through her hair and tipping her head back to meet her sparkling eyes.

"And I think you should," he added with a cocky grin.

Maya's heart was pounding so hard inside her chest, she thought it might explode. She'd never thought to hear anything close to *I love you* from this man, let alone what amounted to a marriage proposal.

And as much as she wanted to stay mad at him for all he'd put her through—not only these past weeks, but the past years—she couldn't. She loved him, too. Truly, madly, deeply, and until the end of time.

He might drive her to distraction at times, but she'd been ready to love him quietly and from afar, just as she always had. Now he was giving her the chance to scream it from the rooftops. And, more, he was telling her he felt the same about her.

Suddenly her eyes filled with tears, and she took a deep, gulping breath, fighting to keep her pulse from galloping out of control.

"Of course I'll marry you," she said in a watery voice, her cheeks growing damp as her emotions spilled over. "I've always loved you, and it killed me to think you'd never see me as anything more than your annoying, unwanted younger stepsister."

"You were always wanted," he told her, his own eyes turning suspiciously bright a second before he pulled her to him and crushed her in his firm embrace. "*Believe me.* I've spent the better part of my life doing my level best not to let anyone see how very much I *did* want you."

She cried into his shoulder for a moment, pure happiness bubbling inside her until it overflowed. "I wish you had said something sooner, instead of making me miserable all these years."

Leaning back, she fixed him with as stern a look as she could manage while all her dreams were coming true.

"Why didn't you?" she demanded, slapping him in the chest. "Even if you couldn't bring yourself to say anything before, you certainly could have said something when we started sleeping together."

He shook his head, a wry smile curving his lips. "Definitely not. I was still deep in denial and only sleeping with you to get you out of my system, remember?"

She arched one dark brow, fighting the laughter that threatened to burst past her lips. "Did it work?"

"Not by a long shot. You were under my skin long before the first time I let myself touch you. But after that, the more I had you, the more I wanted you."

He ran his fingers through her hair again, wiping the trails of wetness from her cheeks with the pads of his thumbs.

"I'll always want you, Maya," he said softly. "And now that I know you love me, too, I'm never going to let you go."

She leaned into him again, her hands at his waist as she absorbed his warmth, strength and love. "Promise?"

"Promise," he whispered, then captured her mouth for a searing kiss.

When they broke apart, they were both struggling for air. Her fingers bunched in the material of his shirt while his ran down her back to cup the curve of her bottom.

"We're going to have quite an announcement to make at Sunday dinner with the family, aren't we?" he said, his hands caressing everywhere they could reach while his lips nibbled at her throat and the sensitive hollow behind her ear.

"Mmm-hmm. How do you think they'll handle it?"

she asked, the smallest trickle of worry wending its way through her bubble of contentment.

Creed lifted his head to gaze down at her, his eyes serious. "I think they'll be surprised, but they're Fortunes—they'll handle it. I also think they'll be happy for us, despite what the media and the outside world might make of our relationship."

She thought about that for a moment, then began to grin. "I think so, too. I can't wait to tell them."

With an arm around her waist, he lifted her off her feet and turned for the bed. "Neither can I, but since Sunday's a couple days off and we just happen to have this nice, soft bed in front of us, I say we make good use of it."

"Oh, by all means," she replied in as serious a tone as she could manage while pure joy coursed through her veins.

Creed tossed her onto the wide mattress, following her down and covering her body with his own. And all she could think was that it had been a bumpy road, with more than a few potholes and pitfalls, but at long last she was exactly where she'd always wanted to be.

She was finally perfectly and deliriously happy, and knew she would remain that way. Forever.

Epilogue

One Year Later

"A toast!" Creed moved around the room, topping off glasses of champagne from the bottle in his hand.

"Uh-uh, none for you, love," he said with a smile, setting down the bottle and handing Maya, who sat on a nearby chair, a glass of punch instead. Before straightening, he leaned in to press a kiss to her forehead and pat the bulge of her hugely pregnant belly.

She was so big now she felt ready to explode. Her husband, however, seemed to love it. He would lie in bed at night, stroking her giant beach ball of a stomach and talking to the baby growing inside.

And anytime she complained about her size, her waddle or the inability to find clothes that both looked good and fit her, he was always quick to tell her how beautiful she was and to remind her that soon—very soon now, since she was a couple of weeks overdue— they would have an adorable baby boy or girl to show for all her discomforts.

Truth be told, she couldn't wait. She was scared and nervous and anxious, but also happy and excited.

This baby would be a living, breathing tribute to her love for Creed, and his for her, and hopefully possess traits that exemplified the best of them both.

They'd been married less than a year, and as Creed had predicted, the press had had a field day when their engagement was announced. He had been wrong about their relationship causing a scandal, however.

The papers and gossip magazines had certainly tried to make a big deal of their being brother and sister, but once it had come out that their only family connection was through the marriage of his father to her mother, with no blood ties between them, the entire story had died down and disappeared within a few weeks.

And, frankly, the Fortune family had begun to get used to the bevy of stories floating around about them, since the frenzy had been going on fairly regularly from the time Nash's and Patricia's lack of a legal marriage certificate had become public knowledge.

They'd had a beautiful, if somewhat hurriedly

planned wedding, and flown off to Jamaica for a luxury honeymoon.

That's where she'd gotten pregnant, to everyone's surprise and delight. Now, if only their reluctant child would decide to make an appearance.

"To Dad and Patricia," Creed continued, breaking into her thoughts as he raised his glass and his voice. "May you forever be as happy as you are at this moment, and may *this* marriage be valid, legal and last forever."

Chuckles spilled through the room, everyone in attendance aware of the circumstances surrounding today's events.

Maya's father, Wilton Blackstone, had been sent to prison for extortion, thanks to Nash and the boys throwing the considerable weight of the Fortune name and reputation behind his prosecution. Knowing that any luck he'd been having had come to a firm and final end, Wilton had also been more than willing to grant Patricia a divorce.

Soon after, Nash and Patricia had started planning a second wedding, where their vows would not only be renewed, but finally, truly legalized.

It had been one of the most talked-about events of the season in Sioux Falls, overshadowing even Creed's and Maya's nuptials, and everyone who was anyone in South Dakota and beyond wanted to attend.

But Patricia and Nash hadn't wanted a big or flashy

wedding, especially this time around. They'd trimmed the guest list down to include only family and a few close friends, and now only immediate family remained, gathering in the great room for a private celebration.

Case and Gina were there, of course, with their six-month-old son, Clive. He was the most adorable thing Maya had ever seen, and she couldn't wait to have one of her own to bounce on her knee and dress in cute little outfits.

Skylar and Zack were also in attendance, making a habit of splitting their time between their home in New Zealand and the Fortune estate so nine-month-old Amanda could grow up knowing her grandparents and cousins.

Max and Diana had also flown all the way from Australia for the occasion, and had dropped hints that they were thinking about starting a family soon, as well.

"Here, here!" everyone agreed in response to Creed's toast.

Patricia laughed, passing her glass of champagne to Nash as little Amanda stretched out her arms, wiggling in her mother's hold as she reached for her grandmother. With a roll of her eyes, Skylar handed her daughter over.

Maya couldn't wait to see her mother holding *her* child like that, but she was happy just to see the contentment on Patricia's face these days. It certainly beat the strain and pallor she'd worn for so long before her first husband had been dealt with and put firmly out of their lives.

Eliza, who was sporting a slight pregnancy bulge of her own, stepped forward and cleared her throat, drawing everyone's attention. Reese stood with her, both with kooky, crooked smiles curving their lips.

"I don't know if this is the right time to make this announcement," she said, "but Reese and I wanted to share the news that…"

Her smile widened as she glanced at her husband. He lifted her hand to his mouth, taking over when she didn't seem capable of finishing. His voice was lower and a bit more controlled, but his pleasure was obvious in the brightness of his eyes.

"We just found out we're having twins."

Cheers and ecstatic exclamations filled the room as everyone rushed forward to congratulate them. Maya shifted back and forth, working to hoist herself up from her seat, which was becoming increasingly difficult these days.

"I've got you," Creed said, appearing at her side to relieve her of her punch glass and pull her to her feet.

"Thank you," she said a little breathlessly.

"You're welcome. Now smile," he cajoled, slipping an arm around the spot formerly known as her waist, "or you'll send poor Eliza into a panic over having to carry two of these."

The idea of being twice as pregnant as she already was sent Maya into a bit of a panic herself, so she did as Creed suggested and planted a wide smile on her face as she waddled forward to add her congratulations to the rest.

After things had calmed down, Nash placed his hands on his hips and focused his gaze on Blake and Sasha, who were cuddled close together, still acting like the newlyweds that they were.

"So," he said, rocking back on his heels. "Everyone else is taken care of. When are you two planning to start a family?"

Sasha blushed to the roots of her auburn hair, but Blake merely shook his head at his father's pushy antics.

"Give us a break," Blake told him, "we just got married."

"And…"

Blake rolled his eyes. "Don't worry, we'll get started on grandkids for you soon enough, I promise. Not that you don't have enough to keep you busy for a while," he added, cocking his head at all the babies and pregnant bellies in the room.

"There's no such thing as too many grandbabies," Nash persisted, his tone gruff despite the happiness of his expression.

Just as the group of Fortunes started to break away, heading for the different chairs and sofas in the room and refilling glasses, a sharp pain slashed low through Maya's abdomen and around her back.

"Oh!" she cried, reaching for Creed, who was right there beside her.

He took her hand, lines of concern bracketing his mouth. "What is it? Are you all right?"

It took her a moment to catch her breath and straighten. "Yes, I'm fine. I think—"

Another pain hit, and she knew she *wasn't* all right. It suddenly occurred to her that maybe the ache she'd had in her back the past couple of days and all of today hadn't been just another fun side effect of her pregnancy, but was actually a sign that the baby's arrival was imminent.

Clutching her belly, as well as Creed's hand, she said, "I think we're about to add another member to the brood of grandbabies."

Chaos broke out around them, but Creed simply swooped her into his arms and strode from the room.

"I can walk, Creed," she complained, knowing she must weigh a ton.

"Hush. I'm carrying my very pregnant wife to the car so we can drive to the hospital and have a baby. Don't argue."

Considering the tightness at her waist and the throb in her lower back, she decided to keep her mouth shut and let him get her to the hospital as quickly as possible.

Behind them, the entire Fortune clan poured out of the house, rushing to their respective cars, strapping babies into car seats and calling out words of encouragement.

Maya took a moment to smile over the flood of family that was about to descend on the local hospital…

and felt more than a modicum of sympathy for the staff there, who would likely be harassed and harangued within an inch of their lives.

"We'll be right behind you, darling," her mother promised, leaning into the car as Creed settled her into the passenger seat and fitted the safety belt around her wide girth. "Don't worry about a thing. We love you."

She kissed the tips of her fingers, then placed them on Maya's brow before stepping back and letting Creed slam the door closed.

Maya's eyes filled with tears and she sniffed.

"Hey."

She turned her head to look at her husband. He started the engine and put the car in gear before reaching over to take her hand.

"Don't cry. I'm nervous enough as it is, and just barely managing to hold it together. If you lose it, we're in trouble."

As always, he knew just what to say. She chuckled and squeezed his hand.

"I won't lose it," she promised quietly. "And I'm nervous, too."

"We'll get through it together, okay? We've also got a hell of a lot of backup," he remarked, sparing a glance for the rearview mirror, where she suspected a procession of Fortune vehicles was trailing behind them.

At the end of the long driveway, he stopped and turned to face her.

"In case things get crazy once we get to the hospital,"

he said, "I want you to know that I love you. I've never once been sorry that I threw caution to the wind and took you as my wife."

She blinked and held her breath, fighting the wash of tears that threatened to spill over. "I love you, too. But if you keep talking like that, I might break down, after all."

He simply smiled, then leaned over to kiss her firmly on the mouth. "Okay. Let's go have a baby."

* * * * *

Watch for Heidi Betts's next book,
CHRISTMAS IN HIS ROYAL BED,
on sale this October from Silhouette Desire.

THE ROYAL HOUSE OF NIROLI
Always passionate, always proud

The richest royal family in the world—
united by blood and passion,
torn apart by deceit and desire

Nestled in the azure blue of the Mediterranean Sea, the majestic island of Niroli has prospered for centuries. The Fierezza men have worn the crown with passion and pride since ancient times. But now, as the king's health declines, and his two sons have been tragically killed, the crown is in jeopardy.

The clock is ticking—a new heir must be found before the king is forced to abdicate. By royal decree the internationally scattered members of the Fierezza family are summoned to claim their destiny. But any person who takes the throne must do so according to The Rules of the Royal House of Niroli. Soon secrets and rivalries emerge as the descendents of this ancient royal line vie for position and power. Only a true Fierezza can become ruler—a person dedicated to their country, their people…and their eternal love!

Each month starting in July 2007,
Harlequin Presents is delighted to bring you
an exciting installment from
THE ROYAL HOUSE OF NIROLI,
in which you can follow the epic search
for the true Nirolian king.
Eight heirs, eight romances, eight fantastic stories!

Here's your chance to enjoy a sneak preview of the first book delivered to you by royal decree…

FIVE minutes later she was standing immobile in front of the study's window, her original purpose of coming in forgotten, as she stared in shocked horror at the envelope she was holding. Waves of heat followed by icy chill surged through her body. She could hardly see the address now through her blurred vision, but the crest on its left-hand front corner stood out, its *royal* crest, followed by the address: *HRH Prince Marco of Niroli*…

She didn't hear Marco's key in the apartment door, she didn't even hear him calling out her name. Her shock was so great that nothing could penetrate it. It encased her in a kind of bubble, which only concentrated the torment of what she was suffering and branded it on her brain so that it could never be forgotten. It was only finally pierced by the sudden opening of the study door as Marco walked in.

"Welcome home, *Your Highness*. I suppose I ought to curtsy." She waited, praying that he would laugh and tell her that she had got it all wrong, that the envelope she was holding, addressing him as Prince Marco of Niroli, was some silly mistake. But like a tiny candle flame shivering vulnerably in the dark, her hope trembled fearfully. And then the look in Marco's eyes extinguished it as cruelly as a hand placed callously over a dying person's face to stem their last breath.

"Give that to me," he demanded, taking the envelope from her.

"It's too late, Marco," Emily told him brokenly. "I know the truth now…." She dug her teeth in her lower lip to try to force back her own pain.

"You had no right to go through my desk," Marco shot back at her furiously, full of loathing at being caught off-guard and forced into a position in which he was in the wrong, making him determined to find something he could accuse Emily of. "I trusted you…."

Emily could hardly believe what she was hearing. "No, you didn't trust me, Marco, and you didn't trust me because you knew that I couldn't trust you. And you knew that because you're a liar, and liars don't trust people because they know that they themselves cannot be trusted." She not only felt sick, she also felt as though she could hardly breathe. "You are Prince Marco of Niroli…. How could you not tell me who you are and still live with me as intimately as we have lived together?" she demanded brokenly.

"Stop being so ridiculously dramatic," Marco demanded fiercely. "You are making too much of the situation."

"*Too much?*" Emily almost screamed the words at him. "When were you going to tell me, Marco? Perhaps you just planned to walk away without telling me anything? After all, what do my feelings matter to you?"

"Of course they matter." Marco stopped her sharply. "And it was in part to protect them, and you, that I decided not to inform you when my grandfather first announced that he intended to step down from the throne and hand it on to me."

"To protect me?" Emily nearly choked on her fury. "Hand on the throne? No wonder you told me when you first took me to bed that all you wanted was sex. You *knew* that was the only kind of relationship there could ever be between us! You *knew* that one day you would be Niroli's king. No doubt you are expected to marry a princess. Is she picked out for you already, your *royal* bride?"

* * * * *

Look for
THE FUTURE KING'S PREGNANT MISTRESS
by Penny Jordan in July 2007,
from Harlequin Presents,
available wherever books are sold.

Silhouette®

Romantic

SUSPENSE

Sparked by Danger,
Fueled by Passion.

Mission: Impassioned

A brand-new miniseries begins with

My Spy

By *USA TODAY* bestselling author

Marie Ferrarella

She had to trust him with her life....
It was the most daring mission of Joshua Lazlo's
career: rescuing the prime minister of England's
daughter from a gang of cold-blooded kidnappers.
But nothing prepared the shadowy secret agent
for a fiery woman whose touch ignited something
far more dangerous.

My Spy

#1472

Available July 2007 wherever you buy books!

nocturne™

**DON'T MISS THE RIVETING CONCLUSION
TO THE RAINTREE TRILOGY**

RAINTREE: SANCTUARY

by *New York Times* bestselling author

BEVERLY
BARTON

Mercy, guardian of the Raintree
homeplace, takes a stand against
the Ansara wizards to battle for
the Clan's future.

*On sale July,
wherever books are sold.*

SNRT2

REQUEST YOUR FREE BOOKS!

2 FREE NOVELS PLUS 2 FREE GIFTS!

Passionate, Powerful, Provocative!

YES! Please send me 2 FREE Silhouette Desire® novels and my 2 FREE gifts. After receiving them, if I don't wish to receive any more books, I can return the shipping statement marked "cancel." If I don't cancel, I will receive 6 brand-new novels every month and be billed just $3.80 per book in the U.S., or $4.47 per book in Canada, plus 25¢ shipping and handling per book and applicable taxes, if any*. That's a savings of almost 15% off the cover price! I understand that accepting the 2 free books and gifts places me under no obligation to buy anything. I can always return a shipment and cancel at any time. Even if I never buy another book from Silhouette, the two free books and gifts are mine to keep forever.

225 SDN EEXJ   326 SDN EEXU

Name	(PLEASE PRINT)	
Address		Apt.
City	State/Prov.	Zip/Postal Code

Signature (if under 18, a parent or guardian must sign)

Mail to the **Silhouette Reader Service™:**
IN U.S.A.: P.O. Box 1867, Buffalo, NY 14240-1867
IN CANADA: P.O. Box 609, Fort Erie, Ontario L2A 5X3

Not valid to current Silhouette Desire subscribers.

Want to try two free books from another line?
Call 1-800-873-8635 or visit www.morefreebooks.com.

* Terms and prices subject to change without notice. NY residents add applicable sales tax. Canadian residents will be charged applicable provincial taxes and GST. This offer is limited to one order per household. All orders subject to approval. Credit or debit balances in a customer's account(s) may be offset by any other outstanding balance owed by or to the customer. Please allow 4 to 6 weeks for delivery.

Your Privacy: Silhouette is committed to protecting your privacy. Our Privacy Policy is available online at www.eHarlequin.com or upon request from the Reader Service. From time to time we make our lists of customers available to reputable firms who may have a product or service of interest to you. If you would prefer we not share your name and address, please check here. ☐

SDES07

THE ROYAL HOUSE OF NIROLI

Always passionate, always proud.

**The richest royal family in the world—
a family united by blood and passion,
torn apart by deceit and desire.**

Step into the glamorous, enticing world of the
Nirolian Royal Family. As the king ails he must find an
heir...each month an exciting new installment follows
the epic search for the true Nirolian king. Eight heirs,
eight romances, eight fantastic stories!

It's time for playboy prince Marco Fierezza to
claim his rightful place...on the throne of Niroli!
Emily loves Marco, but she has no idea he's a royal
prince! What will this king-in-waiting do when he
discovers his mistress is pregnant?

THE FUTURE KING'S PREGNANT MISTRESS

by Penny Jordan

(#2643)

On sale July 2007.

www.eHarlequin.com

HP12643

COMING NEXT MONTH

#1807 THE CEO'S SCANDALOUS AFFAIR—
Roxanne St. Claire
Dynasties: The Garrisons
He needed her for just one night—but the repercussions of their sensual evening could last a lifetime!

#1808 HIGH-SOCIETY MISTRESS—Katherine Garbera
The Mistresses
He will stop at nothing to take over his business rival's company…including bedding his enemy's daughter and making her his mistress.

#1809 MARRIED TO HIS BUSINESS—Elizabeth Bevarly
Millionaire of the Month
To get his assistant back this CEO plans to woo and seduce her. But he isn't prepared when she ups the stakes on *his* game.

#1810 THE PRINCE'S ULTIMATE DECEPTION—
Emilie Rose
Monte Carlo Affairs
It was a carefree vacation romance. Until she discovers she's having an affair with a prince in disguise.

#1811 ROSSELLINI'S REVENGE AFFAIR—
Yvonne Lindsay
He blamed her for his family's misery and sought revenge in a most passionate way!

#1812 THE BOSS'S DEMAND—Jennifer Lewis
She was pregnant with the boss's baby—but wanted more than just the convenient marriage he was offering.

SDCNM0607